ANTHONY PERRY

Chula the Fox

ISBN: 978-1-935684-62-6

Book Design: Corey Fetters
Illustrations: Michael Freeland

Chickasaw Press
PO Box 1548
Ada, Oklahoma 74821
chickasawpress.com

To my late father, Norman Perry, whose absence in my family's life will always be deeply felt.

To my children, Norman and Ilinca Perry, and other Chickasaws who live far from the Chickasaw Nation. Remember your Chickasaw heritage and know that you, in your lives, will continue the Chickasaw story.

- Anthony Perry

TABLE OF CONTENTS

ACKNOWLEDGMENTS

Writing *Chula the Fox* has given me an opportunity to learn about my Chickasaw culture and heritage, things that I took for granted growing up in Oklahoma. I began my research shortly after my father's sudden death in April 2009 as a way to reconnect with him and to better understand the Chickasaw heritage that shaped so much of his life. I found firsthand accounts of eighteenth-century Chickasaw life, such as those by James Adair and Thomas Nairne, but they did not provide a clear view of how my Chickasaw ancestors actually lived their lives and saw the world. I felt that writing a book would help achieve this goal and allow me to better appreciate my ancestors while sharing their story with others. My determination grew following the births of my children. Growing up in England, they will not have the same opportunities that I did to learn about and connect with their ancestors. My hope is that this book will help them to do that.

This book would not have been possible without the steadfast support and patience of my wife, Ecaterina, as I carried out literature and field research. I also owe deep gratitude to my late uncle Charles Perry and my uncles Kirk and Robert Perry, who took the time to answer my many questions about Chickasaw life, both in Chula's time and today.

I also appreciate my friend and former colleague Kate Goddard, who gave helpful and encouraging feedback for an earlier draft of this book.

I could not have found a better home for this book than White Dog Press, an imprint of Chickasaw Press. Thank you to Wiley Barnes, director of Chickasaw Press, for welcoming this book into the White Dog Press family. Thanks also to the editorial team at Chickasaw Press, who came up with great ideas for strengthening the plot and took the time to find answers to my many questions. I thank the Moundville Archaeological Park for all the great work they do to preserve the culture of early Mississippian societies, the likely forebears of Chula's Chickasaw family. I also thank Eric Gilliland, an archaeologist I met at Moundville, who further stimulated my interest in the day-to-day lives of this nation.

Finally, I thank the Chickasaw people for their sense of independence and their fierce determination. I am truly blessed to be part of the Chickasaw Nation.

CHULA the FOX

1 THE HUNT

Red-orange hues of sunlight spilled onto the trail, breaking up the shadows left from the night. A cool breeze brushed my cheek as I looked up through the canopy of leaves, shading my eyes with my hand. We crept along the dirt trail until a rustle in the underbrush caught our attention.

"Be careful, Chula," Uncle Lheotubby whispered. "Don't step on any branches or you'll scare the deer away." I looked down and saw I was standing on a carpet of crunchy brown leaves and twigs. I knew better than to stray from the trail, but I was daydreaming.

"Sorry, Amoshi," I whispered, flashing a sheepish grin at my uncle. I stepped quietly back onto the trail beside my father. Seeing the sunlight scattered between the trees reminded me of the early morning hunts I used to go on with my brother.

I heard a new rustling noise in the brush ahead. Father stopped and reached back toward us, palm out. We stopped, too. Father

1

lowered his hand, signaling us to get ready. We put our decoys over one arm and crouched toward the sunlit field ahead. The decoys were made from the skin of a deer head and neck that was stretched over lightweight cane hoops. They were so life-like they not only fooled the deer, they sometimes fooled other hunters, which meant we had to be even more aware of our surroundings. I gripped my bow, ready to pull an arrow from my quiver. Just ahead of us, a large buck ambled into the clearing, toward a stream in the distance.

Uncle Lheotubby moved his decoy's head side to side, mimicking a deer checking its surroundings. Then we all lowered our decoy heads to the ground as if foraging for food. The buck began to drink from the stream, and we crept forward. Sensing something amiss, he raised his head and listened intently, ears twitching. He soon decided there was no threat and resumed drinking. Our decoys are working, I thought. I crept over near my father, and we all inched closer to the deer.

"Chula, this one is yours," Uncle Lheotubby whispered.

My heart raced. My hands trembled. In one swift motion, I removed my decoy, slotted an arrow against my bowstring, and drew it back. The deer looked up again and froze. I tightened my grip on the arrow and string, making sure they didn't slip through my sweaty palms. My eyes focused on my target, and I let go of the string. *Thwing*! The arrow raced toward the majestic creature. A shriek pierced the morning sky. Leaves and chunks of earth flew as the wounded buck sprinted for the woods beyond the stream.

"I got him!" I shouted.

"Not bad, Chula," Father said. "Come on! Let's find him."

We dropped our decoys and ran, quickly discovering a trail of blood that showed us the way. We followed it through the trees and undergrowth until we found our prey lying on his side with the shaft of my arrow pointing toward the sky. Blood seeped from the

wound, and red froth flowed from his mouth and flared nostrils. He tried to kick his legs, then lifted his head and looked toward us, terrified, before collapsing again and drawing his final breath.

We approached him cautiously. Father bowed his head and thanked Aba Binili for the deer and the continued blessings he gave our family. After a moment of silent reflection, my father knelt down and hoisted the deer over his broad shoulders. He stepped carefully but confidently between the trees, taking care not to do any further harm to the fallen creature.

"Nice work, Chula," Uncle Lheotubby said.

I gathered our decoys and thought about my shot. Each kill made me a better hunter and, ultimately, a better warrior. Every hunt was different. "Just as when fighting an enemy," Uncle Lheotubby often said, "you never know how a deer will react, so you have to be ready for anything." I saw that today.

As we made our way back to camp, Father and Uncle Lheotubby took turns carrying the deer across their shoulders.

"I can help too," I offered.

Father looked at me closely, as if sizing me up.

"This one is still a little too big for you to carry," he said. "Maybe next time."

"You will carry bucks this big soon enough," Uncle Lheotubby said, looking at me sympathetically. I looked straight ahead and nodded slightly. My father was right, though I would never admit it.

I was small for my age. It was Uncle Lheotubby who was always quick to point out my other strengths. I was fast and I was agile, he said. And he was right. I could outrun almost all the other boys in my village and could outmaneuver most of them on the stickball field. But I still wasn't big enough to carry something as heavy as a full-grown deer. Not yet. Not like my brother had been.

My brother had been tall and very muscular, like most of the warriors from our clan. He could carry deer alongside my father and uncle when he was much younger than me. He had been a powerful stickball player and a great hunter and warrior. He was fierce and fearless. Even though he'd been gone for nearly three summers, I still missed him.

By the time we reached the deer camp, several other hunters had already returned, too. The camp was in a clearing in the woods, near a creek that was wide and deep. We'd already been in camp for two days and planned to stay for several more, if we continued to have good hunts. Then we would make the long trek back to our village.

Two women were cooking meat over a fire, while a third woman, Tona, sat dressing the fresh kills and cleaning the hides with her daughters. My friends Nashoba and Osi Waka stood near them, talking and laughing. Hekiubby, the leader of our hunting group, stood up as we approached. "It looks like we've got another deer," he said.

"We do," Father said. "We can thank Chula for this one."

"Well done," Hekiubby said.

"Yakoke, thank you," I said, standing a little straighter and trying not to let the pleasure I felt at the praise show on my face too much.

Hekiubby was shorter than most of the hunters in our group, but he was very muscular and always seemed very serious. Like most Chickasaw warriors, the hair was plucked from his head, except for a topknot of jet-black hair wrapped with a deerskin strap. He had three tattoos on his arms—a snake and a mountain on his right arm, and one symbolizing a river on his left. Each was created from black-dotted marks that ran from his wrists to his shoulders. I knew each of these tattoos signified journeys, perhaps war parties, he had joined. Like most of the warriors in our group, he also had scars on his chest, back, and arms. One especially noticeable scar ran from his right cheek and down onto his neck.

Hekiubby hunted with my father and Uncle Lheotubby often. Father had great respect for him. "I wouldn't go on a raid without him," he once told me. "Enemies underestimate him because he isn't very tall, but they quickly realize their mistake. Hekiubby has no fear and will follow an enemy for days to get his revenge."

He was short *and* fierce. I liked that.

Father placed our buck with the other deer waiting to be dressed.

"That's one of the largest we've had today," Tona said, without looking up from the deer hide she was scraping.

"Chula got this one," Father said. "He deserves the credit."

I smiled and patted the fallen buck's shoulder. "This deer gave me the chance," I said.

Nashoba's sister, Tishkila, rose from where she was sitting and fleshing hides beside her mother. She smiled at me. "I'm sure you had something to do with it, too," she said. "You should be proud."

"Yakoke," I said, "Thank you." I smiled broadly at her.

Before I could say anything more, I felt a hand clamp down on my shoulder.

"What have we here?" His voice was unmistakable—Nukni.

"Chula has made the biggest catch of the day so far," Tishkila said. I thought I detected just a hint of pride in her voice.

"Oh, really? That must have been a sight! A runt like you dragging that big ol' deer back to camp," Nukni cackled. "Must have had a lucky shot."

Nukni was a year older than me and bigger and stronger than most of the boys in the village. He made sure we all knew it, too. Nukni liked to hunt alone and always bragged about his exploits. He usually had a kill to prove his story. Nukni also liked to get into fights, as the scar across his left cheek testified. My friends and I avoided him as much as we could, both in the village and on our hunting trips.

"Where's your kill, then?" Tishkila asked him.

"I'll have mine tonight. Don't you worry," Nukni said confidently.

Osi Waka rolled his eyes at me from behind Nukni, as he and Nashoba came closer to where we stood.

"You don't have a deer yet? We've already killed one each, and it's just mid-day," Nashoba said. "Did your stench scare them off, or did you just miss?"

"Watch your mouth," Nukni said. "You just might lose a few teeth."

"I'm not worried," Nashoba said, stepping closer. Nashoba was almost as strong as Nukni and not afraid of anything. He was usually the first one to call Nukni's bluff.

"Look, even Mahli has a kill," Tishkila interrupted, pointing to the tree line, just as Mahli, his uncle, and another warrior appeared from the woods. They carried two dead deer between them.

"There's two more," Hekiubby said. "It looks like we're going to have a good day!"

Mahli grinned from ear to ear as he came over to join us.

"I think that might be my biggest buck yet," he said.

"So, we all have a kill except Nukni," Nashoba said.

Nukni clenched his fists and stepped toward Nashoba.

"That's enough!" Imonubby, Nukni's uncle, said, grabbing his arm. "You and I are headed back out. You'll have a kill before we return."

Nukni pulled his arm away from Imonubby's grip and glared at us before turning to follow his uncle back into the woods.

"Why don't we go hunt for squirrels and rabbits?" Mahli said.

"That sounds good to me," Osi Waka said. "We can put our blowguns to good use."

I looked at Father and Uncle Lheotubby. "Go hunt," Father said before I could even ask.

"I'm going, too," Tishkila said.

"What about all these hides?" her mother asked.

"I've been cleaning hides all day, Sashki," Tishkila said. "Besides, someone needs to show these boys how to hunt."

"Show *us*?" Mahli said, laughing. "We'll bag far more than you ever could."

"That's not what happened last time," Tishkila said, smiling sweetly. She turned back to her mother. "I won't be gone for long, I promise."

"Fine," her mother said. "Go show them how it's done."

Tishkila quickly retrieved her blowgun and darts.

"Yakoke, Sashki!" she called over her shoulder as she hurried after us into the woods.

•••

The trees grew more dense and the underbrush thickened as we lost sight of the camp. Birds sang in the treetops as the sun began to fall from its mid-day peak.

"Osi Waka, how was your new bow this morning?" Mahli asked.

"It was great," Osi Waka said. "Just the right level of tension in the wood when I took my shot."

"Did you hit your target?" I asked.

Osi Waka smiled. "Right in the throat. The buck dropped straight to the ground. He had no idea what happened."

"Not bad for your first time making a bow," I said.

"You might even become a great warrior like Nukni one day!" Nashoba said, laughing.

"He really thinks he's destined to be a great warrior, doesn't he?" Mahli said.

The truth was, that's what we all aspired to be. All Chickasaw boys wanted to be great warriors. It was our way of life. Most of us just weren't as obnoxious about it as Nukni.

"Maybe he'll even be a great minko, a leader, someday!"

Mahli teased.

"No way!" I said.

"You would hate that, wouldn't you Chula?" Nashoba said.

"Of course I would," I said. "I can't stand Nukni. He always picks on me."

"Why does he give you such a hard time, Chula?" Tishkila asked.

"He always has," I replied.

"What did you do to him?" she asked.

"I don't know." I shrugged and looked at the ground.

I couldn't bring myself to admit it aloud, but I actually did know why Nukni hated me. He told me once.

I had rolled the memory of that day over and over in my head for a long time after it happened, trying to make sense of it. I still wasn't sure I completely understood it.

It had happened on the day my brother got his war name. He and several warriors from our village had returned a few days earlier from battle, victorious. We gathered to honor my brother and the others as they were given war names to recognize their bravery and fearlessness in war.

I was very proud of my brother, but part of me also felt sad. He wasn't a boy like me anymore. Our paths were different now. I wanted to be the one getting the honor, not my brother. My brother knew it. I don't know how, but he did. Afterward, when everyone was gathered around congratulating him, he looked down at me and smiled.

"Your time will come soon, Chula," he said.

I swelled with pride at his confidence in me.

"Yes," I nodded.

Nukni was there and must have heard what my brother said to me, because as soon as the crowd drifted away and my brother went to join the other young warriors in celebrating, Nukni walked up and shoved me, knocking me to the ground.

"What was that for?" I asked.

"Your brother has earned his honor," he said. "But don't think you'll ever get the chance to do the same."

"Why shouldn't I?" I asked. I glared at Nukni.

"Because you're nothing but a runt who thinks he's more than he is—or ever will be."

That was enough. I stood and squared up to him with fists clenched, ready to strike. "Say that again, Nukni. Just try it."

He looked at me and laughed. "The runt of the litter thinks he can teach me a lesson, does he? You're far too small and far too weak to be a fighter."

Then he spat at me and walked away. I should have taken him down right then, but I just stood there. I had been too stunned to even react. Nukni and I had been adversaries ever since.

I shook the memory off as we came to a stop near a fallen tree.

"This looks like a good spot," Mahli said. I settled in on the ground next to Osi Waka to watch and listen, camouflaged by the cover of the tree.

It wasn't long before we heard the unmistakable rustle of a squirrel moving through the underbrush. I grabbed my blowgun and pushed the dart inside it. The thistledown fletching of the dart fit snugly within the hollowed-out river cane tube, ready to fire. A large grey squirrel appeared from the brush and stopped to nibble at the nut he carried.

Nashoba fired his dart first, missing. The squirrel leapt onto the nearest tree trunk and scurried up. Tishkila raced to the other side of the tree and fired her dart. Mahli and I ran up behind her, just in time to see the dart hit its quickly moving target. The squirrel lost its grip and fell to the ground, dead.

"Good shot!" I said.

"More like a lucky shot!" Nashoba said.

"Definitely luckier than yours!" Mahli said.

We all laughed, but we knew it wasn't luck. Tishkila rarely missed her mark. Chickasaw girls usually didn't hunt, but Tishkila was different. She loved to be in the woods hunting or fishing. She loved it so much that her mother just didn't have the heart to keep her from it. The other boys and I laughed at her the first time she insisted on coming along with us to hunt squirrels. We stopped laughing when she bagged more squirrels than any of the rest of us. I still remembered her mother smiling smugly at us when we returned. Most of us were helping Tishkila carry her kills home, rather than our own. Nashoba tried to claim she was such a good shot because he was her older brother, and he had taught her. But that never held water, since he was such a poor shot himself. Now that we were older, she had responsibilities at home that kept her from hunting with us as often as she wanted to.

I grinned at Nashoba and shrugged my shoulders.

"We'll find others," I said. "It's still early."

Tishkila put the squirrel in her pouch, and we continued our search. The birds continued to chirp and sing above us as we moved silently through the trees. Another large squirrel scampered out ahead of us. I raised my hand to signal my friends. We stopped and so did the squirrel. I slowly placed my blowgun to my mouth and prepared to fire. The squirrel looked at us, and then skittered to a nearby tree. As soon as it turned its head, I puffed through the blowgun. My dart hit the squirrel just in front of a hind leg.

The squirrel cried out and ran across the ground, dragging the leg closest to the dart. It clutched a tree with its front claws and desperately tried to climb. I quickly threw my squirrel stick at its head. The short, heavy club hit the squirrel, and the squirrel fell to the ground on its side, motionless.

"That's two," Osi Waka said as I retrieved the squirrel and put it in my pouch. "This is turning out to be a good hunt."

"It is for us," Nashoba said as we continued to look for more squirrels. "I wonder how Nukni is doing?"

"Terrible, I hope," I muttered.

An unusual bird song rang out above us, catching my attention. I looked up and caught a glimpse of the bird's black and white feathers and the red patch on the back of its head as it flitted from tree to tree. The song it sang sounded friendly enough, but I knew deep down it signaled a warning.

"Chula, what's wrong?" Nashoba asked.

"That's a biskinok," I said. Father and Uncle Lheotubby had once described the little bird to me. It was a rarely seen friend who warned of danger in battle. Chickasaw warriors were known to cut short a raid if they heard its call.

We all looked up as it called out '*cheep-ch-ch-ch-ch-ch-ch, cheep-cheep-ch-ch-ch-ch-ch-ch,*' several times in rapid succession.

"We're not at war," Tishkila said. "I wonder what it could mean?"

"It's probably nothing," Mahli said.

They were right. We weren't on our way to battle, but I couldn't shake the uneasiness I felt.

"We should be careful, just in case," I said. We looked around, ready to fire our darts at anything that moved. The biskinok continued its cries as it flew away, deep into the woods.

"I don't see anything out of the ordinary," Tishkila said.

"I don't either," I said. "But I think we should go back to camp just in case."

"I agree," Osi Waka said. "Let's go."

We made our way back carefully, continuing to keep an eye out for signs of danger with each step.

2 THE ATTACK

When we reached the camp, the sun was setting and shadows grew long all around us. Uncle Lheotubby and Father were talking with the women near the fire. I needed to tell Father about the biskinok's warning.

"How did you all do?" Father asked as we approached.

"Not very well," Nashoba said. "We only killed two squirrels between us."

"We had to cut our hunt short, Aki. There was a—"

"You only killed two squirrels?" Nukni's loud, booming voice cut me off as he approached us. He rested his hand on my shoulder, but I shrugged it off. "What did you do, scare them all off?"

"We could have killed more," Nashoba said.

"Sure you could," Nukni said, laughing at us.

"We heard—" I started to say again but stopped. Was it worth telling about the biskinok in front of Nukni? He would just accuse me of making a pathetic excuse for poor hunting. We'd seen no signs of danger. Maybe we were overreacting. I certainly didn't want to give Nukni even more to laugh at.

"You heard what?" Nukni asked mockingly.

"Nothing," I said. "Never mind."

"That's enough, Nukni," Uncle Lheotubby said with raised eyebrows. "I'm just glad you managed to kill a deer this afternoon. Now the other boys won't have anything to tease you about."

"I could have easily killed more," Nukni grumbled. "I just had a bad day."

"Uh huh," Uncle Lheotubby uttered with a smirk, as he turned back to his conversation with Father.

The smell of rabbit roasting on spits over the fire reminded me how hungry I was. Mahli and I claimed some of the rabbit meat and sat on the large rocks near the edge of camp to eat. As we ate, I watched, taking comfort in the familiar rhythm of hunting-camp life.

Darkness had fallen, and groups of hunters were clustered around small fires scattered throughout the camp. Some seemed deep in conversation about the day's hunt or other important matters. Others sat in comfortable silence, cleaning muskets or repairing arrows. Tishkila had joined the women who were clustered around the main fire, talking and laughing as they cooked and tended to the hides. Nashoba and Osi Waka were playing some sort of game with a group of boys at the far end of the camp.

I heard a commotion in the woods behind me. I turned to look. In the darkness, I could just barely see two of our warriors as they broke through the tree line, running as fast as they could go. One of them was shouting, but I couldn't make out the words. I finally heard the word "Choctaw!" just as an arrow slammed into the tree trunk next to us with a *Thwack*! Then, the loud crack of a musket rang out, and one of the hunters standing near the edge of the camp cried out and fell backwards.

Mahli quickly slid behind the rocks we were sitting on, grabbing his bow and reaching for an arrow in his quiver, which was still slung over one shoulder. I instinctively lurched toward the spot where I had last seen Father and Uncle Lheotubby. Everything seemed to move in slow motion.

I felt someone grab my arm and tug me toward the tree line. It was Uncle Lheotubby.

"Chula! This way!" he yelled. As I turned to follow him and Father, I saw an enemy warrior running toward the main fire—and the women. He held a knife in his hand. As he raised his arm to strike, Tona reached up with one swift motion and tore through his abdomen with the long knife she used to gut the deer. Hekiubby and another man ran past her, leaping over the fallen warrior, to intercept his friends who seemed to be pouring into the camp now.

Father, Uncle Lheotubby, and I quickly took cover behind a fallen tree trunk in the woods just outside of the camp clearing. I kept watch behind us, with my bow in hand, as Father and Uncle Lheotubby defended our position and the camp. Father rose up from behind the trunk to fire his musket, then Uncle Lheotubby took over, using his bow to deliver arrows with deadly force while Father reloaded. I wiped the sweat and dirt from my brow and prayed for Aba Binili's protection.

More arrows and gunshots sliced through the air around us. I peered over the trunk and saw dark figures dashing from tree to tree in the woods.

Father rose up again to fire another shot. I heard him cry out and looked up. He was clutching his left shoulder. Dark blood spilled out from between his fingers. He clenched his teeth to avoid making more noise.

"Chula, give us cover!" Uncle Lheotubby said.

I took up a new position, keeping watch in front of us and behind, as Uncle Lheotubby examined Father's shoulder. "It's pretty bad, Pisatubby," he said. "Hold the wound tightly, and we will cover it as soon as we can."

Uncle Lheotubby took Father's freshly loaded musket and fired again. In the distance, I heard more shouting. It seemed to be moving away from us. Uncle Lheotubby and I watched and waited, our weapons ready to fire at any sign of enemy movement. At last, the woods fell silent. Glimmers of moonlight scattered across the forest floor.

"Are they gone?" I asked.

Uncle Lheotubby stood silent for a moment, listening intently to the woods around us. Then he nodded. "I think so, Chula. Keep a sharp eye on those woods for me, just in case they're not."

He carefully picked through the pouch on his hip and took out a rolled-up strip of hide. Father held his breath as Uncle Lheotubby wrapped it tightly around his wounded shoulder. "This should stop the bleeding."

Father nodded and clutched the bandage tightly.

Both Father and Uncle Lheotubby froze at the sound of a bird call from deeper in the woods. It wasn't an owl, but a songbird of some kind. The sound seemed out of place in the darkness of night.

"That is Hekiubby," Uncle Lheotubby said. Uncle Lheotubby sounded out a call of his own. Other calls followed.

"They're telling us—" Father coughed before he could finish. Uncle Lheotubby raised his hand to stop Father.

"They're telling us the camp is secure," Uncle Lheotubby said. "We're to stay where we are and guard this side until daylight."

We waited in silence, listening carefully for any sign of the enemy returning. My heart raced with each breath. The camp was secure for now, but who knew if they would return? I wondered who else was hurt—or worse.

•••

When the first rays of sunlight finally broke the darkness, I looked around to try to get a better sense of what happened. Father was resting against the fallen tree trunk we'd taken cover behind. His shoulder was caked in blood, despite Uncle Lheotubby's bandage, and he was obviously in pain.

Uncle Lheotubby had sat at Father's side all night, tending to his wound and watching for any sign of the enemy. He had dried blood on his chest too, which I thought may have come from Father. I looked down and saw scratches across my own chest and arms from the thick, thorny underbrush we had run through. Now that I had noticed them, I began to feel the sting from the cuts.

I heard the same unusual bird call from the night before, quickly answered by three other calls that seemed to come from different parts of the forest.

"It's time to go," Uncle Lheotubby said, getting up from the ground. "The others will meet us there."

We both helped Father navigate the underbrush, taking care not to put too much pressure on his injured shoulder.

When I caught sight of the camp, I had flashbacks to last night's attack and a mixture of fear and dismay washed over me. The fire that had warmed and sustained us just last night was now a pool of black, charred wood and gray ash splashed across the ground. A bloodied handprint settled into one of the few deer hides that remained nearby. I saw several motionless bodies scattered around the camp. I knew some of them. We had laughed together just yesterday, and now they were dead. Tears welled up in my eyes.

"Amoshi, why?" I asked.

Before Uncle Lheotubby could reply, a voice behind me said, "*Why* is not as important as *who* right now. We will make the cowards who attacked us pay for this." It was Hekiubby. Two other grim-faced warriors, Obiyachatubby and Chufatubby, stood next to him, along with Tona, Tishkila, and Nashoba.

Father swayed slightly and reached for Uncle's arm to steady himself.

"We'd better take care of your shoulder," Uncle Lheotubby said.

He carefully sat Father against a tree and removed the bandage. Tishkila brought water for Father to drink, and Tona moved to help Uncle Lheotubby clean and rebandage the wound.

As they worked, Father looked up at Hekiubby.

"Where's Ayakubby?" he asked, gritting his teeth against his discomfort.

"He's tracking them," Hekiubby said. "When he returns, we will know more."

A strange look passed between them. Father nodded.

"There," Uncle Lheotubby asked as he finished securing a new piece of hide around Father's shoulder. "How does that feel?"

"I am fine," Father said. "I just need to get up and stay on my feet." He got to his knees but nearly fell over as he tried to stand. He groaned and clutched his shoulder even more tightly.

"I think you'd better sit back down, Pisatubby," Hekiubby said. "Take some rest."

"I don't think I have a choice," Father said.

"No, you don't," Obiyachatubby said, shaking his head.

Another group of hunters filtered into the camp. I was relieved to see Osi Waka and Mahli with them. Two of the hunters had dried blood on their faces and another had a bandage on his leg, similar to Father's. Osi Waka was covered in mud from head to toe. He looked as confused and frightened as I felt.

"I am glad to see you all," Hekiubby said.

Tona motioned the bloodied and bandaged hunters over to one side of the camp where she and the other women were tending to the wounded.

"How many have we lost?" one of the hunters asked Hekiubby.

"We have four dead here in the camp—two men and two women—along with two dead Choctaws," Hekiubby said. "And we have several still unaccounted for, including Nukni and Imonubby."

"Then we'd better start looking for them," Obiyachatubby said. "Let's spread out in pairs."

"I will stay with Father," I said.

"No, Chula," Father said. His voice was starting to sound strained. "Go and help find them."

"We will stay with Pisatubby," Tona said. She looked over at Tishkila, who nodded and smiled at me reassuringly.

"What if the Choctaws are still out there?" Osi Waka asked. We all turned to look at him.

"They aren't," Sahkubby said. "Onahubby and I tracked them with Ayakubby until we were sure they left the area. They were running like scared children."

Osi Waka nodded slowly, reluctantly accepting Sahkubby's reassurances.

"All right, then. Let's go," Hekiubby said.

At that, we parted ways. I went with Uncle Lheotubby into the woods on the other side of the camp. I thought about Nukni. I didn't like him, but I didn't want him dead. As we walked, I tried to make sense of the attack in my head. We weren't at war and, as far as I knew, no one from our village had had any problems with Choctaws recently. I knew unprovoked attacks happened sometimes, but this just seemed to go against everything I knew of honor and justice. It didn't make sense.

We continued walking between the trees, looking carefully for any sign of our missing hunters. Birds flew overhead, flitting from tree to tree, and squirrels scampered across the ground, oblivious to our plight. I thought about the cries of the biskinok.

"Uncle Lheotubby, I need to tell you something."

"Tell me what?" he said.

"I think we were warned about the attack," I said.

"What do you mean?" Uncle Lheotubby stopped and looked at me.

"When we were hunting squirrels yesterday," I said, "a biskinok cried out above us. I think it was trying to warn us."

"Why didn't you say anything?" he said.

"I was going to, but Nukni was giving us a hard time so I waited. And then the Choctaws attacked us before I could tell you." I looked at the ground.

"Not many people get to hear the call of a biskinok," Uncle Lheotubby said. "They often warn of danger. You should always take heed when you hear one. You're inexperienced in such things, though, and we weren't expecting trouble."

His words weren't meant as a rebuke, but they stung nonetheless.

We continued through the woods in silence. As we came over the top of a hill, I saw someone in the distance. It looked like he was on his knees, hunched over something in front of him that I couldn't see. I glanced at Uncle Lheotubby, and he made a gesture to be quiet.

We held our bows ready, just in case it was an enemy, and cautiously made our way over. As we approached, I recognized Nukni. A motionless body lay in front of him. My heart dropped.

"Nukni?" Uncle Lheotubby called out.

Nukni looked up. We lowered our bows and moved closer. His face was pale, the lack of color made even more pronounced by the dark mud smeared on his cheeks. He breathed deeply. His uncle

Imonubby lay before him.

"My uncle is gone," Nukni said. His eyes welled up, but he did not cry.

"What happened?" Uncle Lheotubby asked. My heart sank with a familiar pain. Nukni didn't deserve to lose his uncle.

"We chased the enemy this far. He killed several of them," Nukni said, "but he ended up getting shot himself."

Uncle Lheotubby rested a hand on Nukni's shoulder. "Chimoshi was a brave man and a powerful warrior," Uncle Lheotubby said. "Aba Binili will give him peace."

•••

When we returned to camp all eyes were on us, but no one spoke. Uncle Lheotubby and Nukni gently laid Imonubby's broken body with the rest of our dead.

Hekiubby stood up and approached us. "It's good to see you, Nukni," he said. Nukni opened his mouth but struggled to respond. He finally gave up and just nodded.

"We found Nukni sitting next to him," Uncle Lheotubby said as the rest of our group gathered around. "He was shot in the attack."

"Everyone else has been accounted for," Obiyachatubby said. "We lost too many souls."

"Even one is too many," Father said. He coughed, gripping his shoulder. It seemed to be bleeding again.

"Revenge is due," Sahkubby said angrily.

"I'll see to it myself," Hekiubby said. "But first, we owe our fallen brothers and sisters a dignified rest. Let's give them this and get our wounded home. Then, we will plan our revenge."

We quickly built platforms for the bodies of those we lost. We hacked the branches off of small trees with our knives and lashed the poles together with long strips of deer hide. Then we placed each body atop a platform, so that they looked skyward with their arms to their sides. We covered them with logs to protect them from birds and wild animals. The families of the dead would come back later to retrieve the bones of their loved ones and take them home for burial.

Once we were finished, we said a short prayer to Aba Binili and carefully loaded our remaining supplies and pelts onto our boats. We then pushed off from the blood-stained banks of the creek and began the long journey home with heavy loads, heavy hearts, and much anger in our souls.

3 THE DARKEST NIGHT

Nukni had been silent since we left the camp. As we neared our village of Ayanaka he finally spoke. "We're almost home and I—" He stopped. I looked over at him in the canoe alongside ours. He took a slow, deep breath. "I don't know how to tell my family Amoshi is dead."

I remembered the day Father came home from a raid without my brother. Worry and confusion had filled my heart as soon as I saw him and Uncle Lheotubby come over the hill—alone. Then I saw the sorrow in Father's eyes.

"He's gone," Father had said as his voice broke. "He is with Aba Binili."

Mother, my little sister Pakali, and I had rushed toward him and Uncle Lheotubby, trying to make sense of what happened. Mother and Pakali screamed and pounded against Father's chest as he stood in silence. Now, Nukni would have to give similar news to his family. For perhaps the first time ever, I felt sorry for him.

Hekiubby, who sat behind Nukni, rested his hand on Nukni's shoulder. "I will go with you," he said.

Nukni nodded. He took another deep breath and quickly brushed his arm across his eyes.

As we paddled our canoes further along the creek, clusters of homes came into view on the ridge above us. Ayanaka, like most Chickasaw towns or villages, was spread out along a ridgetop. We were almost home. Our group began to disband as the men landed their canoes near their homes. Mahli raised a hand and said goodbye as he and his uncle veered toward the bank. A little further on, I watched as Tishkila gathered her things and scrambled up the bank after Nashoba and her parents. At last, I could see our home in the distance.

"Lheotubby, will you and Chula need help getting Pisatubby home?" Hekiubby asked.

"Don't worry about me," Father said, clutching his bloodied shoulder. Father looked tired, though I could tell he tried to hide it.

"Chula and I will look after him," Uncle Lheotubby said. His voice was calm, but his eyes held a sense of urgency.

Uncle Lheotubby helped Father out of our canoe and together we supported Father as he hobbled to the top of the ridge. Mother stood outside the summer house, near the brush arbor, stirring the food inside a large clay pot with her pashofa paddle. Grandmother and Aunt Ohaiki sat on mats under the shade of the arbor, weaving baskets from river cane. Mother looked up and smiled when she saw us coming. When she realized Father was leaning into Uncle Lheotubby for support, her smile dissolved. She quickly hung the pashofa paddle on the arbor post and ran toward us.

"Pisatubby!" she called out. "What happened?"

"We were attacked at the hunting camp," Uncle Lheotubby said as we helped Father toward our summer house. "Pisatubby was shot."

Father did his best to reassure her. "I'm all right, Kayohe," he said, clearly exhausted. I wanted to believe him, but I knew he was hurting. He had started to cough blood on the trip home, and his breathing had become more labored. He didn't complain, but I could see the weariness on his face. His jaws clenched in pain with every step he took.

As we neared the house, Pakali ran outside and threw her arms around Father's waist with a hug that forced a pain-filled grimace from him. "Aki! You're home!" she shouted. Pakali's deep brown eyes twinkled, and she gave a smile that could warm the coldest heart. Father forced a big smile.

"Chukma, hello, Pakali," he said.

"Pakali, let go of chiki," Mother said. "He's hurt."

Pakali let go and looked up at Father. "I'm sorry."

"It's okay, my little flower," he said. "I'm glad to see you, too."

Father lifted his hand to stroke her hair just as his knees buckled. Uncle Lheotubby was still by his side and managed to keep him from falling to the ground.

"Get him inside," Grandmother ordered.

Mother and Uncle Lheotubby helped Father settle onto his bed. Grandmother unwrapped his blood-stained bandage. Aunt Ohaiki quickly filled a bowl with water and washed the blood from his wound. Grandmother covered the wound with yarrow leaves and wrapped it in a fresh bandage. Father's eyes were still closed. Grandmother placed her hand on his face. "He feels feverish," she said, turning her eyes to Uncle Lheotubby. "Tell me what happened."

As Uncle Lheotubby described the attack, I looked down at Father. His eyes looked sunken and his skin was ashen. He breathed quick, shallow breaths. I was afraid. Would we lose him like we lost my brother and like Nukni lost his uncle? I took his hand and squeezed it tightly. Despite the fever, his hand was cold. I prayed to Aba Binili and asked for protection.

Mother looked worried, increasing the fear I felt. Father began to shiver, so Mother covered him with a deerskin. His breathing grew shallower, and he coughed violently, leaving sprinkles of blood on his chin and arm.

"Chula," Uncle Lheotubby's voice was low, but urgent, "we need the alikchi, the doctor. Go, get him—quickly!"

I turned and sprinted toward the healer's home at the other end of the village. As I entered his yard, he was coming out of his house. We nearly collided.

"Chula, what's wrong?" he asked.

"Aki's been shot," I wheezed, trying to catch my breath. "He's getting weak. He needs your help."

"Let's go see him," the alikchi said. He gathered his bag of herbs and medicines and called his assistant over. They followed me home.

•••

Mother met us in the yard. The alikchi nodded at her and went inside. From just outside the doorway, I could see Father. He looked like he was still asleep, but I knew it was worse. Sweat glistened on his brow, and his skin had a tinge of purple around his eyes and mouth. The alikchi would tend to him alone. Everyone else huddled together outside. The solemn expressions on the faces of the adults confirmed my deepest fear. Like my brother, Father might die.

"We will do our best to help," the healer's assistant said, "but it is ultimately in Aba Binili's hands." Mother sat near the arbor, holding Pakali in her lap. Tears streamed down their cheeks. I turned away just as a lone tear rolled down my own cheek.

I could hear the alikchi praying quietly, and I knew he knelt next to Father's bed. I moved to a spot where I could see into the house through the open doorway. I watched as the alikchi rose from Father's bedside. He took a small clay bottle from his bag and rubbed ointment across Father's forehead. He then took a small clump of herbs, crushed them in his palm, and made a paste that he spread over the wound. Father groaned.

I trembled as the alikchi raised his arms over my father and called for Aba Binili's help. I wanted to make Father whole again, to make him better, but there was nothing I could do but watch, hope, and pray.

Finally, the assistant came to the door and motioned us inside. Sobs from Mother and Aunt Ohaiki filled the room. A dark emptiness fell over me like a blanket, and everything around me blurred. I wondered if this was how my Father felt when he found my brother dying. Did the same hopelessness, the same sense of desperation that overwhelmed me now, overwhelm him too?

Just as things had seemed to move in slow motion when we were attacked, they seemed to move too quickly now. "Chula," I heard Uncle Lheotubby say, "ch*i*ki is with Aba Binili and the spirits of our people now. He has joined your brother."

My legs trembled so violently I could barely stand. Mother knelt next to Father and embraced him. Pakali cried.

"*Aki!*" I said. He lay motionless. I touched his forehead. It was cold. Tears streamed down my cheeks. My father was dead.

"We'll need to prepare him for his rest," Grandmother said quietly.

Mother wailed again and kissed Father's cheek. Then she slowly looked up at me and Uncle Lheotubby. More tears fell down her cheeks, and she took a deep breath. Seeing Mother and Pakali in so much pain tore my heart. My own sorrow was deep, but with each new cry from my mother and sister something else began to well up in my chest, too. It was anger. Anger at the men who caused this. Anger at the men who had killed my father and robbed my mother of her husband. Anger at the men who taken my sister's father from her. Silently, I vowed to make them pay.

Mother slowly pushed herself up from the ground. "I'll get some water so we can bathe him. Pakali, you and chiposi, your grandmother, come with me." She motioned to the alikchi, "You come too."

When they left, I looked at my uncle. "How could this happen?"

"Chiki was a strong man, Chula. But Aba Binili calls even the strong home when we least expect it. The wound was more than his body could take."

Mother returned. "The alikchi has done all he can. Now he will help us prepare my husband for the spirit world." Mother shut her eyes and took several deep breaths, as if to steady herself.

"Come, Chula," Uncle Lheotubby said. "We have a long night ahead of us."

I knew we would need to dig a grave for Father. Following Chickasaw custom, we would lay him to rest under the floor of our home. We began to dig into the hard dirt floor near Father's bed. The dirt refused to give way at first, but we pushed our way through until we reached the softer soil below. As we dug, Mother and Aunt Ohaiki washed Father's body. Mother cried softly as she wiped the blood from his shoulder.

"We're going to get through this," Aunt Ohaiki whispered, putting her arm around Mother.

I heard wails in the distance and knew others in our village were in mourning as well. The cries grew closer, and soon a group of warriors, friends of my father, came through the doorway followed by their wives. I was surprised and relieved to see

Nashoba and Mahli with them.

Uncle Lheotubby nodded a greeting at the other men as they joined us in digging. The women consoled Mother and joined in helping to prepare Father's body for the burial. The alikchi stood over Father's body and prayed quietly.

By the time we finished digging, we had a mound of dirt taller than me in our house. A deep pain filled my stomach as I looked down into the dark hole where my father would soon rest. I looked around and saw the others talking but couldn't hear what they said. My ears buzzed, and my vision blurred again. The pain was too great. I could do little more than watch and try to keep out of the way.

Mahli and Nashoba were beside me, talking in hushed tones. A hand touched my shoulder. "Chula," Nashoba said. His voice was faint and seemed to echo in my mind. "Chula," he said again, shaking me gently this time.

I turned to look at him.

"Your uncle needs you," he said, pointing.

I followed his direction and saw Uncle Lheotubby watching me from across the room. He raised his eyebrows and made a circular motion in the air with his hand. I nodded. It was time for me to gather Father's favorite things so he could take them with him to the spirit world.

I grabbed his hunting bow, his quiver of arrows, and his musket from where they rested beside the door and placed them next to the hole. Nashoba and Mahli followed close behind, silently offering their support. Pakali came over from where the women were preparing Father's body. Seeing me gathering items, she went to her things next to her bed and walked back toward me, cradling an object against her small body.

"Can Aki have this, too?" Pakali asked. As she got closer, I saw it was a corn husk doll Father had made for her. It was Pakali's favorite toy.

"I'm sure he would like that," I said. I smiled at her and, for a moment, she smiled back at me.

Her innocent smile, laced with sadness, was almost more than I could bear. In that moment, I decided on my own tribute for Father. I took my knife out, knelt beside Pakali, and asked for her help. Together we cut off the braid that fell down my back, even with my shoulders. Pakali tied the freshly cut end with a strip of leather, and I added my braid to the items to be placed in Father's grave. Even with most of my hair gone, I didn't feel any lighter.

I stepped outside for some fresh air. I glanced toward the women and saw Father seated on a bearskin rug. I took a deep breath as I looked closer. He was wearing a fresh breechcloth, deerskin leggings, moccasins, and his favorite bear-tooth necklace. Mother painted his face red in the traditional fashion of Chickasaw warriors, but without the black marks that symbolized war and death.

"Your husband was a powerful warrior," Aunt Ohaiki told Mother. "Aba Binili will greet him well."

Mother called the men outside. We all gathered around Father and bowed our heads. My father sat peacefully, as if he were merely resting his eyes. Despair washed over me as I realized I would never see him awake again. I would miss our hunting trips, the stories he shared of his childhood, and the advice he gave me on how to get Uncle Lheotubby to go easy on me when I did something wrong. Father's earthly journey had come to an end, and I had to move on without him.

"Let us lay our friend, our father, and our husband to rest," the alikchi said. He anointed Father with bear oil, placed his hands on Father's forehead, and offered another prayer. "May you bless Pisatubby, dear Aba Binili. Give his spirit strength and rest, for he was a loving father and a valiant warrior who gave his all for his family and his people. May we never forget his love, his strength, and his courage."

Mother looked at Father in the firelight and cried. Pakali stood next to her, clutching Mother's hand, tears streaming down her face, too.

Uncle Lheotubby put his hand on my shoulder. "It is time. Will you help us carry him?"

"Yes, Amoshi."

Uncle Lheotubby and I stood around Father's body with four other men and prepared to lift him. I held his right arm and shoulder, opposite Uncle Lheotubby. The other men took hold of Father's chest and legs. Together, we lifted him and held him so he reclined upon our shoulders.

"Come," the alikchi said. We slowly turned to face him where he stood before the entryway to the house. The women, now wailing much louder, stood behind us in a single line. Their cries tore through my already weary heart.

We followed the alikchi around the summer house, keeping the house to our right. When we reached the entryway again, we turned toward it and paused. We walked around the house two more times, pausing each time we reached the entryway. The third time we paused at the entryway, and we prayed.

We entered the house and approached the grave. At the alikchi's direction, we lowered Father into his grave, his majestic face illuminated by the flickering light of a nearby torch. Mother carefully handed us Father's bow, arrows, and musket. Uncle Lheotubby and I laid them beside him, and I placed Pakali's doll and my braid in his lap.

"It's time to let him sleep," the alikchi said. The women's cries grew louder. I helped Uncle Lheotubby and others fill the grave with dirt until we could climb out.

As we continued our work from the floor above, I looked over and saw Mother's grief-stricken face in the firelight. I paused. Noticing my hesitation, Uncle Lheotubby said, "Chiki will rest with your brother. He will be well."

I hoped my uncle was right but I feared otherwise. Father himself had said that those killed at the hands of their enemies would wander the earth until they found justice. My father's suffering had just begun.

As they left, the alikchi and the warriors and their wives bowed their heads and gave us one final goodbye. Nashoba and Mahli both gave me a half-hearted slap on the shoulder as they followed their families out the door.

When they were gone, I turned to Uncle Lheotubby. "I will find them," I growled. "I will find the men who shot Aki and destroy them, even if it costs my last breath."

Uncle Lheotubby looked back at me for a long moment. He seemed to be considering something. "In time, Chula," he said. "In time."

4 CRIES FOR REVENGE

I couldn't sleep. Every time I closed my eyes, I saw my father. I saw him coming home from a long hunting or trading trip as I ran toward him. I saw him in the golden sunlight, spearing a giant fish in Chiwapa Creek with me and Uncle Lheotubby. I saw him smile with great pride after I shot the deer on our last hunting trip together. Then, I saw his lifeless eyes gazing toward the sky from his bed, motionless and cold. I saw him being lowered into his grave, and I heard Mother and Pakali wailing in despair.

The enemies' war cries echoed in my ears as I remembered how quickly they appeared from the woods, overtaking us like a swarm of ants. I thought about the dead bodies I had seen strewn about the camp. I thought about Father getting shot and how I prayed that he wouldn't die. But then he did.

"How could this have happened?" I asked myself. Across the room, Mother turned on her bed and then settled back to an uneasy sleep. The enemy dared to kill Chickasaw warriors, the fiercest warriors ever. They killed my father. They would not get away with it. We would have justice.

As the rage began to swell in my chest again, I knew trying to sleep was useless. I needed to run. I got out of bed, grabbed my bow, and slipped out into the night. I ran toward Chiwapa Creek, guided only by the cloud-laced light of the full moon. I crossed the creek and ran toward the silhouettes of the large trees that loomed ahead. I could hear coyotes yipping in the distance.

I reached the tree line and continued on. Slivers of moonlight lit the forest floor, just bright enough to help me see a faded trail ahead and to the left. I knew every stone, every tree, and every twig on every trail in these woods, but I couldn't remember this trail. I joined it, not caring where it took me. I ran on and on, and before I knew it, the darkness began to fade. Birds woke from their nighttime slumber and called out to each other. It was Father who taught me how to recognize their different voices. I heard a robin calling out *we-we-we, teee-teee, we-we-we, teee-teee,* over and over again. Another answered in the distance. Then, a mourning dove called out *who-llliioouu, who-who,* followed by the raucous call of a blue jay. A new day was beginning.

I climbed a large, grassy hill and came upon a shimmering pond. The calm waters glowed with the pink and blue hues reflected from the rising sun. A large, silvery fish leaped up near a grove of cattails by the shore and splashed back down, leaving a ripple of expanding rings in its wake. I sat down on a large boulder that overlooked the pond. I looked down into the water and watched several streamlined sunfish nibbling on strands of algae. As I watched, I realized that the swirling grief and rage had, for a moment at least, eased. I was suddenly exhausted. I struggled to keep my eyes open. I leaned over, rested my head on my folded arms, and closed my eyes, drifting gently into the darkness that followed.

I felt something touch my shoulder. I sat upright and froze, wide-eyed. Standing next to me was an old man half my size. "You were sleeping soundly, Chula," he chuckled.

"Who are you? And how do you know my name?" I asked.

"I know you well, Chula," the old man said as he sat down next to me on the stone. I shivered. Grandmother often told stories of *i*yaknasha, the woodland spirits known as little people. Sometimes they meant well, but other times they played tricks on those they visited.

"We always look after your people," the little man said softly. "I know ch*i*ki passed into the spirit world last night. I am sorry for your sadness."

This one seemed to mean well. "Yes, *A*ki is gone," I said after a pause. I fought to keep my voice steady.

"Ch*i*ki was a fierce warrior. Even when injured, he never stopped fighting."

He did know my father!

"They attacked us like cowards," I said. "I swear I will avenge his death."

"Chula, ch*i*ki is with the spirits now," the old man said. "Your family needs you. You must be strong for them."

"How does that help *A*ki?" I asked. "How will that bring peace to Sashki and my sister?"

"Keep strong, Chula. Look after your family, and they will find peace. Remember ch*i*ki, and you will find your path." A breeze twisted by, carrying a cloud of whirring insects near my left ear. I shook my head and swatted at the flies. When I turned back, the little man was gone.

"*A*ki's death will *not* go unanswered," I said bitterly. I got up, faced the warmth of the morning sun, took a deep breath, and headed home.

When I reached the edge of our yard, I stopped. I could hear Mother talking to Aunt Ohaiki inside our house. She sounded angry. I crept closer to listen, keeping out of sight of the front entrance.

"It's not just the death, Ohaiki, it's the senselessness of the fighting. There's no honor in this, no justice." Mother's voice cracked with emotion.

"Pisatubby was a brave man and a loving *i*ki," Aunt Ohaiki said. "We're all going to struggle to fill the void he's left behind, but we will pull through this."

Mother's anger and sorrow cut deep into my heart. I crept closer to the door and peeked inside. Aunt Ohaiki sat next to Mother with a comforting arm around her shoulders.

"I don't know what to do," Mother said after she caught her breath. "First my son, now my husband. I'm afraid for more loss, Ohaiki. I'm afraid for Chula."

I edged closer. My foot knocked against Mother's cooking pots stacked between me and the wall, making a loud banging sound. Mother stood quickly, wiping the tears from her face with the back of her hand.

"Chula! You startled me," she said. "Where have you been?"

"Just out in the woods," I said. I thought about the little man and considered telling her but decided against it. Grandmother said the *i*yaknasha didn't like it when you talked about them.

Mother hugged me tightly. "I'm glad you're here now," she said. "Are you hungry?"

I nodded, and she handed me a bowl of the pashofa that was warming over the fire.

"It looks like we're just in time to eat, little one" Grandmother said, as she and Pak*a*li swept through the door. "It smells wonderful, Kayohe." She tried to sound cheerful, but she couldn't entirely erase the sadness from her voice. Pak*a*li tried to keep a brave face, too, but her red, puffy eyes and tear-stained cheeks betrayed her.

"Come here, Pakali," Mother said, wrapping my sister in a tight hug. Pakali leaned into the hug and caught her breath so she wouldn't cry, but her tears fell nonetheless.

We tried to find things to talk about as we ate, but finally gave up and finished in silence. Filled with pashofa and too exhausted to fight sleep anymore, I crawled onto my bed and closed my eyes.

•••

"Chula," Grandmother said, poking me. I looked around and tried to clear the grogginess from my head. Late afternoon shadows filled the room.

"Aposi?" I asked. "What's wrong?"

"Everything is fine, Chula." Grandmother assured me. "It's time for us to get ready for tonight. Why don't you run along and find something to do?"

Tradition dictated Mother and some of the other women would mourn at each dusk and dawn for the next twelve full moons. Then the time for mourning would be over, and we would have to move on.

I did as Grandmother asked and wandered out into the woods near our house. I listened to birds and watched squirrels chasing each other in the trees until the sun lowered into a deep orange pool on the dark horizon. Wisps of gray-streaked clouds washed in purple brushed the sky above it. As darkness fell, so did my heart.

When I returned home, I saw the women coming out of the house in a line. Grandmother called out a deep, mournful cry, chanting to the heavens for Aba Binili's strength and support. Mother, Aunt Ohaiki, and Pakali joined her, creating a fervent choir of sadness. A coyote howled in the distance, followed by several more. Their mournful cries mixed with the sobbing of the women. The women circled our home three times, pleading for peace and mercy in raised voices.

Their mourning was more than I could bear. I slipped away and headed for the center of the village. Uncle Lheotubby and the council were meeting tonight. They would be planning our response to the attack. I had to find out for myself what that plan was. I had to be a part of it.

As I approached the council house, I could hear the voices of our warriors raised in fierce debate. I slipped inside silently and saw Nashoba, Mahli, and some of the other boys, including Nukni, standing in the shadows at the back of the council house.

"What did I miss?" I whispered to Nashoba as I joined them.

"Ayakubby has returned. He knows where the Choctaws who attacked us live," Nashoba said. "They're trying to work out when to attack. Some want to send warriors tonight, but others want to wait."

The warrior's voices grew even louder, drawing our attention back to the debate.

"We owe it to our fallen brothers to crush the enemy now," one of the warriors said. It was Hakalotubby. He was fierce—sometimes too fierce. Father and Uncle Lheotubby said he was impulsive and often rushed into a fight before he thought.

"If we go now, they will be expecting us," said Hekiubby, who was seated near Tushka Homa, the minko, our leader. Hekiubby's red skunk family, Inkoni Homa, was among the most respected in our village for their bravery.

"Hekiubby is right," Uncle Lheotubby said. He sat between Hekiubby and Tushka Homa. "We want vengeance, not more dead Chickasaw warriors. If we bide our time, we will be able to regain the element of surprise. They won't expect us to wait."

"They will think we are weak if we wait," Hakalotubby argued. "They attacked a peaceful hunting party without provocation. We must respond swiftly."

"Hakalotubby is right," another warrior said. "Our lost ones demand vengeance. Each day that passes leaves them calling us more urgently for justice."

"That is a pain we must bear for now," said Tushka Homa. "We must think with our heads as well as our hearts, or we will have even more fallen warriors calling to us for vengeance. We will wait."

"How long do we wait?" Hakalotubby asked, his displeasure at the idea of waiting still evident.

"We will know when it is time. Our patience and cunning are weapons just as powerful as our might," said Anowatubby, another powerful warrior who my father respected greatly. All of us boys had heard the stories about Anowatubby's bravery in battle. He earned his war name, which meant "He walked around there killing," many years earlier in a fight against a band of Cherokee who attacked him and three others as they went to trade with the English in Charles Town.

"If we wait, they could raid our village next," Hakalotubby said. "Do we want to put the lives of our women and children at risk?"

"I agree," Obiyachatubby said. "An attack on our homes is a risk we can't take."

"I saw their village. Their numbers are small," Ayakubby said. "They do not have the men they would need to attack a Chickasaw town and survive."

"Attacking a Chickasaw town would certainly be foolish," Uncle Lheotubby said. "But then, they haven't shown the best judgement up to this point. That shouldn't keep us from waiting until the right moment to strike back. We can post lookouts to watch for invaders."

"They will expect us to seek vengeance quickly," Anowatubby said. "But if we wait until after the harvest, their guard will be down. They will think we are not coming."

"Do you mean you want us to wait for six whole moons to pass before we do anything about this?" asked another warrior who had been silent up to this point.

"That's far too long!" Hakalotubby protested. "I'll go and attack them myself before then."

"Not in our name, you won't," said Uncle Lheotubby. "They'll kill you and be more likely to attack us."

"I like Anowatubby's idea," Hekiubby said.

"Anowatubby's suggestion is sensible," Tushka Homa said. "Can the rest of you agree to this?"

There were rumblings and some raised voices as the council members discussed the matter among themselves.

"We'd better do it now," Nukni said angrily, from the crowd of boys standing behind me.

"Be quiet," another boy whispered. "You want the council to hear you?"

Nukni scowled but grew quiet. None of the warriors seemed to have heard his outburst.

Tushka Homa rose and the council members grew silent. "It is decided," he said. "We will attack the enemy after the harvest. In the meantime, we will prepare our young ones to fight alongside us."

Nashoba and Mahli looked at me with wide eyes. Our chance to prove ourselves as warriors might come sooner than we thought.

"I'd better get home," I told Nashoba. "Amoshi will be going there to update everyone, and I don't want to miss anything."

I ran home along the moonlit trail, my mind flooded with thoughts of war and revenge. Suddenly a glowing light appeared in front of me. I stopped and stared, not believing my eyes. The light hovered in place. I cautiously approached it. Slowly, it began to take on the form of a man, bathed in light. I looked more closely, confused. He reached toward me. A chill trickled down my spine as I realized the man looked like my father.

"Aki?" I said. "Is that you?"

The glowing figure began to twist as if made of smoke and disappeared.

I stood frozen in place for a few moments staring at the place where the light had been. I tried to make sense of what I had seen. It had to mean something. Or maybe I was still just suffering from exhaustion and grief. That must be it, I decided. I was just imagining things. I shook it off and went on home.

When I got there, several women were still sitting with Mother, brushing her hair and consoling her. Pakali came over and gave me a hug. "I miss Aki," she said. Her voice seemed to echo.

"I miss him, too," I said after a pause.

Soon, Uncle Lheotubby arrived.

"How was the council meeting?" Grandmother asked. "Do you know why we were attacked?"

"No, we don't," Uncle Lheotubby said.

"This attack cannot go unanswered," Mother said. Her eyes flashed with anger. "What will the council do about it?"

"Ayakubby has returned. We know where they came from. Rest assured, Kayohe, we will see justice. We will strike them so fiercely they'll pray for the comforts of death."

"When? And who will go?" she asked. The anger in her voice seemed to have changed to something else I couldn't quite put my finger on.

"We are going to wait until after the Green Corn Ceremony— let them believe we have forgotten. It will also give us time to prepare our boys," Uncle Lheotubby said.

"Lheotubby, no!" Mother said.

"Kayohe, we can't stop them from becoming men. It will happen sooner or later. It is the way things are meant to be."

"I want to go, Amoshi," I said, quickly. "I want to fight, to avenge *Aki*."

"It won't be easy, Chula. You are young, and you still have much to learn," Uncle Lheotubby said, studying me gravely.

"*Aki*'s dead, and he calls out to me. I hear him now." I looked toward Father's grave and wiped a tear from my eye. "I am ready to be a warrior, a warrior like *Aki*."

"Chula, you're just a boy," Mother said. "There's no reason to grow up before it's time. Let chimoshi and the others seek justice for us."

"I am not a boy! Not anymore," I said bitterly. "And I *will* give *Aki*'s spirit rest."

"Chula—" Mother started, but Uncle Lheotubby held up a hand to silence her. I could see the anguish in her eyes, but I could not agree to do what she asked.

My breath quickened and my legs trembled. "Sashki, even you can't stop me."

"Chula, calm down," Uncle Lheotubby said quietly. He gently rested his hand on my shoulder.

"I will fight, Amoshi," I said. "I have to."

"That remains to be seen," he said and looked at Mother. "He will prepare with the others," he said firmly.

Then he fixed his eyes on me. "You will have to work hard to earn the approval of the warriors. Going on a raiding party is not a game, and it is not a place for boys. It is the work of men. If you go, we will depend on you for our very lives, Chula."

"Yes, Amoshi," I nodded.

Mother breathed deeply and then let out a rush of air. "And I'm depending on you, Lheotubby." They locked eyes for a moment, then Mother turned and left the house with Grandmother and Pakali trailing behind her.

5 CATCHING DINNER

A fog of grief surrounded our house over the coming days and weeks as we tried to rebuild our lives without Father. He lived on in my dreams each night. I often saw him smiling and laughing with us along the creek or over a meal by the fire. Sometimes, though, I awoke with the shock of a reverberating gunshot and my bed soaked in sweat. All I had to do was look across the floor at Father's grave to know that our loss was real.

Mother continued to push us on. "Chula," she said one morning, "I want to have fresh fish tonight with cornbread. Go to the creek and see what you can catch. While you are out you can set the snares, too. If we're lucky, we'll have a rabbit for stew."

"Sure, Sashki," I said. "I'll see if Nashoba or any of the others want to come along."

"I'm sure they'd like that," Mother said.

"Can I go, too?" Pakali asked.

"No, I need you here to help me with the hides. We'll have to go to the market soon to sell them." Mother said.

The disappointment on Pakali's face was obvious, but she didn't say anything.

"Sashki, I haven't gotten to spend much time with Pakali since Aki died. It'd be great if she could come along to help," I said.

"Maybe Nashoba can bring Tishkila, too," Pakali added. It was hard to ignore the excitement in her voice.

"All right, then," Mother said. She shook her head and smiled. "Go with your brother. I need to see chishkosi, your aunt, anyway. I'll see if she can help. You can help me tomorrow."

"Yakoke, Sashki!" Pakali said.

"Come on," I said. "You get the snares, and I'll get the fishing gear."

"I really hope Tishkila can come," Pakali said as we headed out.

"You mean, you really hope to see her outfish the boys, don't you?" I said, raising my eyebrows at her.

She thought about it, and then grinned and nodded slightly. "Maybe," she said. We both laughed, then fell into a comfortable silence, admiring the lush green leaves bursting from the ash, oak, and elm trees around us as we walked toward Nashoba's house.

We were nearly halfway there before Pakali broke the silence.

"Chula, are you really going to go fight?" she asked.

"I hope so," I said.

"Are you afraid?" she asked.

I took a deep breath and thought about that for a moment before answering her.

"Uncle Lheotubby says every good warrior has a little fear. He says it keeps them sharp," I finally said. "So maybe I am. But, I think I'm more afraid of not fighting. Of not getting justice for Father and the others."

I could feel the familiar mix of anger and grief swirling inside me at the thought of Father.

"I just wish we were going now instead of waiting," I added.

Pakali frowned. "Grandmother thinks the council's decision to wait is good. She said being patient and watching for the right time to act has always served us well in war. She said it is part of what makes our warriors so feared."

As we reached Nashoba's yard, I thought about what Pakali said. What could Grandmother have meant? How could patience and waiting make warriors fearsome? I would have to ask Uncle Lheotubby about that later.

By the time we headed into the woods, our group included Osi Waka, Nashoba, Mahli, and Tishkila.

As we picked our way through the brush, Tishkila said, "I hope we don't see another biskinok this trip."

"We're too close to home," Nashoba scoffed. "No one would be dumb enough to attack us here."

"I don't know," Osi Waka said. "My father thinks they might. He said the Choctaws that have allied with the French to the south are a threat to us."

"My uncle says the same," Mahli said. "He's agreed to be one of the lookouts in case they do come."

I looked over at Pakali, who seemed to grow more anxious as she listened to all our talk.

"My Uncle Lheotubby doesn't think they will," I said. "He said the band that attacked us just saw an opportunity, with us away from the village and all, and took it. They won't come here, where they are sure to be defeated."

"I hope your uncle is right," Osi Waka said.

We all grew silent as we ambled deeper into the woods. Three rabbits jumped across the trail in front of us. We froze. They were young rabbits, and they couldn't be far from home. They darted off the trail down a steep hill. Leaves, fallen branches, and moss blanketed the bottom—the perfect spot for a rabbit hole.

"I bet we'll find a good place to lay a snare down there," I said.

I took one of the sinew and bark-fiber twine snares, climbed down the hill, and nestled the snare by the tree. I then set it and covered it with a handful of grass and leaves.

"That should catch a rabbit," Pakali said.

"I hope so," I said.

We set a few more snares in the same area. "We shouldn't go much further than this, since we'll have to check them each day," I said.

"We could set the others over here," Nashoba said, pointing to the dense woods on the other side of the trail.

"That's perfect," Osi Waka said. We picked our way through the trees and set the remaining snares in place.

"Even if we don't catch rabbits," Mahli said, "we should at least get some squirrels or maybe even a turkey."

"We'll find out soon enough," I said. "In the meantime, let's catch some fish."

We made our way to the creek. The waters were wider here than at home. Bass, sunfish, and catfish of all sizes passed by in the clear water.

"Looks like they're going to make it easy for us today," Tishkila said.

Pakali stood on the bank and watched as the rest of us raised our spears and entered the creek.

"It just takes one good shot," I told Pakali. I waited patiently until a large bass blithely swam past me. I thrust my spear into the water. The fish writhed violently as the spear landed in its mottled, olive green side. "Got him!" I called out.

Pakali cheered. "Well done!"

"Help me put him into the basket," I said. The slippery fish struggled as I lifted it out of the water. Pakali opened the basket, and I shook the fish off my spear.

I returned to the water, and we waited for it to settle. We raised our spears again as more fish swam toward us. Osi Waka signaled that he was ready to strike. He hurled his spear into the water, not letting go, as another fish flailed beneath the surface.

"Here's our second catch," he said, pulling the fish out of the water. Pakali opened Osi Waka's basket, and he put the fish inside.

We continued to catch fish until everyone had several in their baskets. Of course, Tishkila's basket was the fullest.

"This is too easy!" Nashoba said. "Let's make it more challenging."

"How?" Tishkila asked.

"Just watch," Nashoba said, laughing.

He put his spear on the sandy bank and waded across the creek toward a rocky ledge that extended over the shore on the other side. He crouched down until the slowly flowing water reached his shoulders, and then dove beneath the ledge.

He stayed underwater longer than I expected. I grew worried. "We'd better see what's going on," I said.

We walked toward the ledge but stopped as he burst above the surface with a large, black catfish flailing desperately between his hands. "Now this is fishing!" he said.

Pakali was delighted. She clapped her hands and laughed. "Well done! You caught a fish with your bare hands!"

Nashoba walked past us with the still-flailing fish and placed it in his basket. He smiled smugly at Tishkila. "I guess I didn't teach you everything I know," he said. She wrinkled her nose at him.

"My turn," I said.

I waded into the water and slowly approached the ledge, taking care not to scare any other fish that might be lurking beneath. Then I closed my eyes, took a deep breath, and plunged myself underwater. I shoved my arm deep into a dark crevice beneath the ledge and waved it back and forth. I could feel the resistance

of the water swirling around my arm as it changed direction. Suddenly, my arm pulled away from me. I jerked it back and grabbed my assailant by its mouth with my free hand. The fish flailed and I nearly lost my grip. Holding on tight, I lunged toward the surface with the fish in hand.

"What do you think of this?" I asked, laughing in triumph. My catfish was even bigger than Nashoba's.

"Now, *that's* a lucky catch," Mahli said.

"A catch is a catch, all the same!" I said. I climbed out of the water, still holding the fish tightly so it wouldn't wriggle free. Pakali opened the basket and I put the fish inside with the others.

"I can't wait until *Aki* sees—" I said, and then stopped, realizing my mistake. The afternoon had been so normal, so like things were before Father died that I had forgotten just for a little while.

Pakali looked at me with sympathetic eyes, and I wondered if things would ever truly be that way again.

6 MARKET DAY

A few days later, we all went to the market to trade. I loved our trips to the market. People came there several times each year from places far and wide to trade. Sometimes there were people from places I'd never even heard of. There was always something new to see, to taste, and to touch among the goods at the open-air market that was hastily set up along the creek bank.

We set out just after sunrise, walking along the long, rocky trail surrounded by prickly pear and small shrubs to the market spot. Our horse, Heloa, carried baskets of produce from our garden and some of Uncle Lheotubby's deerskins.

The market was a hive of activity. We saw baskets of sweet potatoes, vibrant red strawberries plump enough to burst, and lush herbs used for everything from making tea to curing stomachaches. One trader had beautiful, large white and pink shells gathered by the tribes who lived along the great salt waters in the east, and another had fish from the stream nearby, some so fresh they still flopped in their baskets. There were a variety of clay pots and baskets, each with its own distinct style and use. There were also items that could be used for adornments, like copper, obsidian, and colorful feathers from birds I had never seen before. White traders brought cloth, metal pots and tools, knives, and muskets.

As we walked along the market, I saw a group of boys my age playing marbles. Each boy tried to get his small, stone marble closest to the marker within five rolls. I paused to watch for just a moment, until Mother called out for me to keep up.

When we reached Mother and Aunt Ohaiki's usual spot, Uncle Lheotubby, Pakali, and I helped them set up. As soon as we finished, our baskets of yellow squash, long green beans, and plump potatoes attracted attention. We were quickly surrounded by curious customers.

"Lheotubby, why don't you and Chula go wander around for a while?" Mother said. "I'll look after everything here with Ohaiki."

"All right," Uncle Lheotubby said. "Come on, Chula. Let's go."

We browsed along a row of trade goods until Uncle Lheotubby stopped at a trader with several bows on display. "These could be worth a closer look," he said.

Each bow was carefully carved from hickory and oiled with bear grease to keep them limber. Beneath the bows were small baskets filled with arrowheads of different sizes. The smaller ones were used to hunt rabbits and squirrels, while the larger ones could kill deer or even enemy warriors if needed.

I brushed my hand against one of the larger bows. My fingers glided against the smooth wood in one stroke, without a single bump or splinter. I looked up at Uncle Lheotubby. "Amoshi," I said. "I think I need a bigger bow. Could we get one?"

"Don't worry, Chula, your bow is fine for now. These bows are too big for you. We'll get you one like this when you're a bit older."

"Why are they too big?" I asked. "Mine will kill a deer, but I don't think it's strong enough to finish the enemy who killed Aki. I need one that will."

"A big bow like this won't do the job for you. You're not strong enough yet to shoot the shot you need."

I didn't want to hear that. "So, what do I do to become a good warrior then? You promised you'd show me how to fight."

"Listen to me. I did promise to teach you how to fight, and I will." Uncle Lheotubby rested his hand on my shoulder. "For now, let's see what else there is to look at."

As much as I wanted to argue, I knew I wouldn't win. "All right, Amoshi," I said, grudgingly.

"I could use some more arrowheads," said Uncle Lheotubby. "Why don't you pick the ones that will give us the best of luck?"

I dug into one of the baskets, picked ten arrowheads, and showed them to Uncle Lheotubby. He picked them up, one by one, for closer inspection.

"Well, these four look good," he said. "The others don't look as sharp as they should be, and one of them has a faint crack. Have another look and find more like these four."

I returned to the basket, looked through the arrowheads again, and carefully chose six more. "How are these, Amoshi?"

"Much better," Uncle Lheotubby said. "We'll make a fine hunter of you yet." Uncle Lheotubby then agreed on a price of four small amber beads with the trader and put the arrowheads in a deerskin pouch he carried with him.

We passed by a few other traders but stopped when we saw a white trader selling muskets, along with cotton fabrics and glass beads. "Hello," he said with an English accent. "Come and see the finest offerings from the civilized world."

Uncle Lheotubby grunted in response, then looked at me and

rolled his eyes. I grinned back at him. He always acted like that when the white traders used the word "civilized" to describe themselves. I wasn't exactly sure what the word meant, but it seemed as though they were trying to say they were somehow better than Chickasaws. Whatever it was, Uncle Lheotubby obviously didn't agree with them.

We quietly browsed through the man's things. "Let me take a look at that gun," Uncle Lheotubby said, pointing to one of the smaller muskets propped up against a makeshift wooden stand.

"Of course," the trader said, "here you go."

"It isn't loaded, is it?" Uncle Lheotubby asked.

"No, of course not," the trader replied.

Uncle Lheotubby examined the gun closely and brushed his hand along the barrel. He then turned away from the crowds and aimed the gun as if he was about to shoot. "It looks to be in good shape," he said. "The barrel feels smooth, and I don't see any warp to the wood. It's lightweight. Perfect for a good hunt."

"It is," the man said. "It's a flintlock musket, made in England. It's far better than what you get from the French. You're lucky the shot doesn't blow up inside the barrel with one of those." A chill ran down my back when he said this. My brother died when his gun exploded during a raid. I thought back again to when Father came home without him.

"That's good to know," Uncle Lheotubby said. He then inspected the flintlock, which was used to ignite the powder and fire the gun. "Well, this looks to be in good shape, too. Chula, why don't you take a look?"

"Sure," I said, not quite knowing what to expect. I had seen Father with his gun, but he never let me touch it.

Uncle Lheotubby carefully handed me the gun. "Take it with both hands, and hold the barrel upwards toward the sky," he said. I held the gun, admiring the smooth, brown, wood stock.

"How does it feel?" he asked.

"It's very light."

"Yes, it is. Now, turn around and aim it toward those trees, away from any people," he said. I did as he instructed. I could just about imagine a large deer or a bear lumbering in those woods. I peered over the barrel and put my finger on the trigger, as if I were about to fire. "Yes, just like that. So, how does that feel?"

"It's easy to hold. It feels natural," I said.

"How much do you want for it?" Uncle Lheotubby asked.

The trader placed his hand on his furry chin. "Well, I'm always looking for good deerskins. You don't happen to have any, do you?"

"I do. We brought top-quality deerskins with us. They're with my wife. Why don't you come with us and see for yourself?"

"I'm trading alone today, and I can't leave my spot. Why don't you bring me thirty good skins, and we'll call it a deal?"

"That's a lot for a gun. Other traders we have passed by are offering guns for twenty skins."

"Show me what you have, and I'll see what I can do," the trader said.

"All right, hold that gun. We'll be back," Uncle Lheotubby said. "Let's go, Chula."

I couldn't believe Uncle Lheotubby was buying me a gun! I looked at him in disbelief as we made our way back to Mother and Aunt Ohaiki. "Yakoke, Amoshi!" I said.

"It's time you had a gun of your own, Chula," he said. "I promised you I would teach you how to fight, and I will. I know it's what chiki would have wanted."

By the time we reached them, Mother, Aunt Ohaiki, and Pakali had traded away most of their harvest. "Well done!" Uncle Lheotubby said. "So, what did you get in return?"

"We did well, Lheotubby," Aunt Ohaiki said. "We have glass beads, some new bowls and—"

"And four pigs!" Pakali said, grinning.

"Yes, and four pigs," Mother said, smiling at Pakali. "Two of which we can eat, and the other two can start a family of their own. We won't be running out of pork anytime soon."

"Good plan. I'm sure Chula and Pakali will enjoy that. Chula and I had a good day as well, in fact." Uncle Lheotubby rested his hand on my shoulder and smiled.

"Well, I'm guessing that explains the silly grin on Chula's face?" Mother asked.

"It does. He also picked out some good arrowheads. Your husband taught his son well."

"Yes, he did," Mother said, with a touch of sadness in her voice. She smiled at me.

"We're getting something else, too, but I need the deerskins we brought with us," Uncle Lheotubby said.

"What are you getting?" Aunt Ohaiki asked.

"You'll see. First, let me take those deerskins. We'll be right back."

"How mysterious," Mother said and winked at Pakali.

Uncle Lheotubby slung the deerskins over his shoulder, and we walked back to the white trader.

"These are the skins, as promised. Take a look and you'll see they're top quality," Uncle Lheotubby said as he carefully laid the skins onto the ground.

The trader knelt down to inspect them one by one. He stroked each, and then turned them over to check the underside. "These aren't bad at all. The leather is smooth and the hides are thick."

"As I said, those skins are top quality. I'll give you twenty for *that* gun."

The trader carefully returned the skins to Uncle Lheotubby. "They're good, but I'll need more than twenty for that gun. It was handcrafted with great care, so it will last. You can see that in the

intricate carvings and the polished wood. I couldn't let that gun go for less than thirty of those deerskins."

"It's going to be hard for me to part with all of them," Uncle Lheotubby said. "I could give you twenty-five, though."

"I tell you what," the trader said. "You're going to need more than the gun itself to make it useful. There is the shot, black powder, and paper. I'll give you enough of those to get you started if we agree on thirty skins for the gun."

Uncle Lheotubby rubbed his chin and furrowed his brow as he studied the gun. I held my breath, waiting to see if he would change his mind and walk away. Finally, he dropped his arms to his side and said, "All right, thirty skins for the gun and plenty of ammunition."

The trader extended his hand and Uncle Lheotubby shook it. Then he gathered the balls, paper, and black powder and put them in a leather pouch for us. "Here you go. Good luck!"

"I'm not the one you should be giving that gun to," Uncle Lheotubby said. "It's my nephew's gun."

Joy raced through my heart. I slowly reached out to take the musket from the trader. When it rested in my hands, I held it as carefully as an egg. I had my own gun, and I wasn't about to let it get even a scratch. "Yakoke," I said.

"You're welcome, boy," the trader said.

We started back toward the spot where we'd left Mother and Aunt Ohaiki.

"You had better take good care of that gun, Chula," Uncle Lheotubby said. "I don't have enough deerskins to spare to get you another."

"I will. I promise," I said.

"Good. Before long, I'll have to show you how to use it. Did you ever see chiki shoot his gun?"

"Yes, but I wouldn't know how to fire one myself. It looks hard."

"It's not too hard, once you get used to it. We'll go hunting with it soon, so you get comfortable."

"I want to kill more than deer with it, Amoshi," I said.

Uncle Lheotubby stopped and looked at me, his brow furrowed. "I know, and you will. First, we'll start with deer, then ducks. Then you'll be ready to hunt what you're really after."

"I want to give Aki peace," I said. "I still hear his voice in the night. He doesn't rest."

"He will, Chula," Uncle Lheotubby said. "Above all, know that he wants you to be at peace. He wanted nothing more for you when he was alive, and that didn't change when he died."

"I know. And I can't be at peace until I avenge his death," I said. My pulse thumped in my head and I trembled. "I will fight to my last breath if that's what it takes."

"In time, Chula," Uncle Lheotubby said. "In time. For now, let's find chishki and chishkosi!"

When we reached them, Mother and Aunt Ohaiki were packing the last of their things. Pakali played with a doll nearby.

"Well, what have you got there, Chula?" Mother asked.

"It's a brand-new musket. My very own!" I said. "Amoshi promised he'd teach me how to shoot with it, and I'm going to get even—"

"You're going to learn how to hunt, Chula," Uncle Lheotubby interrupted. He looked at me sternly. "Aren't you?"

"Yes. Amoshi is going to teach me how to hunt."

"Every young warrior needs a gun, and it's time Chula learned how to use one," he said.

Mother packed the last of her bundles onto Heloa as she looked intently into Lheotubby's eyes. "I will blame you if something happens to him."

"Chula will be fine," Uncle Lheotubby said.

The trip home was quiet. Dusk slowly turned into darkness as we reached the village.

I lay in bed that night thinking about my new musket. I had my own gun, just like Father. I couldn't wait to learn how to use it, and Uncle Lheotubby was going to show me how. I drifted off to sleep with a smile on my face for the first time in a very long time.

7 LEARNING TO SHOOT

U ncle Lheotubby came to get me a few days later. "Chula, are you ready to try that new musket out?" he asked as he stood in our doorway.

"Yes!" I exclaimed, springing up off the floor where I had been working on a new set of blowgun darts. I scrambled to collect my musket and ammunition.

"Chukma, Kayohe," Uncle Lheotubby said to Mother.

"I'm well, yakoke," Mother said without looking up from the basket she was weaving. I glanced over at her. Her face was stern, but not angry. As far as I knew, she and Uncle Lheotubby hadn't discussed my participation in the raid since the night of the council meeting. As her older brother, it was Uncle Lheotubby's place to direct my upbringing, especially when it came to things like this. I knew she wouldn't directly oppose him. I also knew she worried about me, and she wasn't pleased with the idea that I might fight in battle so soon.

She didn't say anything else to Uncle Lheotubby, but as I headed out the door she said, "Be sure to check the snares while you're out, Chula."

"Yes, Sashki. I will," I said over my shoulder.

"Let's do that first," Uncle Lheotubby said as we stepped outside into the bright sunshine.

We walked along the well-worn trail to the spot where I had set our snares. I slid down the crescent-shaped embankment toward the first set of snares and found a rabbit in one.

"Not bad," Uncle Lheotubby said. "Check your other snares and see what else you've got."

As I worked my way through the other snares, I gathered another rabbit and a squirrel. "We're going to have a feast with these!" I said excitedly.

"Well, maybe a stew, anyway," Uncle Lheotubby said, squinting skeptically at the small rabbits. "Let's head over to that clearing over there, and I'll show you how to use your musket."

Uncle Lheotubby pulled out an old, worn rabbit pelt. "Go wrap this around the tree over there. It will be our target."

The tree was about a hundred paces away. I attached the pelt to its trunk.

"Good," he said. "Now do exactly as I say. Do you understand?"

"Yes, Amoshi," I replied.

"This gun can either save you or kill you, depending on the care you give it."

"I will be careful. I promise."

"Good," he said. "First you need to inspect the gun. Make sure there isn't dirt or anything else around the trigger or along the barrel." He inspected both parts on his gun, and I did the same on mine. Uncle Lheotubby then stood the gun up from the ground and held the barrel. "Now, we need to make sure the inside of the barrel is clean. It has to be clear of any obstructions so you can load and fire the shot safely."

"Okay," I said.

"Watch me and do as I do." Uncle Lheotubby pulled out the rod that ran underneath the barrel. I did the same. He slid the rod inside the barrel of his gun. "Make sure the rod runs smoothly against the barrel. If you feel any rough spots, we'll need to clear them."

I slid the rod down inside the barrel of my gun. "Everything seems fine," I said. "The rod went in smoothly."

He nodded. "Now, we need to make sure the flintlock is ready. Take your gun like this." Uncle Lheotubby held the gun level. "Open the lid here on the top, and make sure the compartment is clean inside."

I did as I was told. "I see some black powder there. Is that okay?"

"Yes, that's fine, if it's just a little," he said. "Go ahead and wipe it with this, so it's as clean as possible."

I took the pelt he handed me and wiped away the powder. "Done," I said.

Uncle Lheotubby took my gun and inspected the flintlock. "That looks good. Now let's prepare the ammunition." He gave my gun back to me, and we opened our ammunition pouches. Inside were sheets of paper, several small but heavy balls, and a bag of black powder. "Now, do as I do."

Uncle Lheotubby took out a sheet of paper and laid it flat onto the ground. Then, he folded the paper into a small tube, pinched the bottom shut, and stuffed it with an ammunition ball and black powder.

I did exactly what he had done. "Does this look right?" I asked.

"That's fine," he said. "Just close off the top part of the paper like you did at the bottom and you're done." He patted me on the back as soon as I sealed the top of the pack. "Great work, Chula. Let's make a few more." When we finished, we had eight shots each in our ammunition pouches.

"That wasn't hard at all," I said.

"Once you know how, it's easy," he said.

We each picked up our guns and stood up.

"Hold the gun along your waist like this so it points straight ahead. Then, push this lever down until it clicks." He watched me until I had pushed the lever.

"Good. The gun is what is called 'half-cocked.' Now, open the lid for the compartment you cleaned earlier."

I flipped up the cover and exposed the pan.

"Take one of the shots you put together and tear open the top part, like this." Uncle Lheotubby took one of his shots with one hand and bit the top part, ripping it from the paper case. He spat the piece of paper from his mouth.

I tried to do the same, but some of the black powder stuck to my tongue. It had a bitter, metallic taste. I spat it out as soon as I could. "That tastes horrible!" I said. "How do you keep black powder from spilling inside your mouth?"

"Lots of practice and great care," he said, chuckling. "Don't eat too much of it, Chula."

"I won't," I said. I spat again to get rid of any remaining trace of the powder.

"Now, you need to open the plate on top of the gun and pour some of the black powder inside—not a lot, but enough to cover the bottom, like this." Uncle Lheotubby poured a small amount of black powder into the container beneath the plate and closed the lid.

I tried to do the same, but had trouble opening the plate.

"Push it back, like this," he said. He put his hand over mine and pushed on the plate.

I poured some of the black powder inside like he did and closed the lid.

"Now, shove the rest of the shot down the barrel." Uncle Lheotubby put the end with the black powder in first and pushed it inside. "Once that's done, pull out the rod from beneath the barrel and shove it as far down inside as far as you can."

I could feel the edge of the rod pushing the ball and paper wad farther inside. "I think it's in as far as it will go," I said.

Uncle Lheotubby nodded.

"Hold your gun like this." He raised his gun against his shoulder and pointed it toward the pelt tied around the tree. I held my gun like he did and pointed it at the pelt.

"Now, push that lever down another notch."

The lever settled into place with a clicking sound as I pushed it down.

"When you're ready, brace yourself and pull the trigger," he said as he demonstrated. *WHOOOM!* A peal of thunder ripped through the barrel of his gun, followed by streams of fire and puffs of smoke. He lowered his gun and looked at me. "What are you waiting for? Take your shot."

I looked back at the tree and adjusted my aim. As soon as I pulled the trigger, the back of the gun kicked hard against my shoulder and knocked me to the ground, flat on my back. My ears rang with the echo of gunfire, and my lungs filled with smoke.

Uncle Lheotubby grinned broadly and reached out his hand. He said something to me, but I couldn't hear him over the ringing in my ears. I took his hand and rose to my feet. I rubbed my shoulder and my ears until the ringing sound stopped. "Good shot!" he said.

"Yakoke," I said.

"Let's try again. This time, make sure you stay on your feet!"

I reloaded, aimed at the pelt, pulled the lever, and then the

trigger. *WHOOOM!* Two puffs of gray smoke floated above my gun, and another ripple of thunder tore through the air. This time, I stood my ground.

We fired off two more shots each. "Let's see how we did," Uncle Lheotubby said.

There was one hole through the pelt and two fresh chunks missing from the trunk above it. "It looks like a few shots missed, Amoshi," I said.

"I'm not surprised, Chula. These guns don't always hit where you aim them. It takes a lot of practice and even more luck, I'm afraid."

"So, we really didn't do too badly then, did we?" I asked.

"No, we didn't. We'll have to practice a lot more, though. Your gun should feel as natural as your own hands."

"It doesn't feel that natural yet," I said, shaking my head. I wasn't sure it ever would.

"You'll get there. It just takes time and practice." Uncle Lheotubby rested his gun on his shoulder. "For now, let's get you home."

When we arrived, we were greeted by the scent of roasted pork and corn. "Something smells wonderful," Uncle Lheotubby said. "What is that?"

"Fresh stew," Pakali said, smiling up at him.

"And it's almost ready," Aunt Ohaiki said. "It looks like you've brought some food yourself."

"Yes, from Chula's snares," Uncle Lheotubby said, handing the small game to Mother.

"A messenger came by looking for you, Lheotubby. The council is meeting this evening," Grandmother said.

"I'll have to eat quickly then," he said.

"Will they be talking about our revenge, Amoshi?" I asked.

"Yes, Chula, I believe so," he said.

Pakali gave us bowls and horn spoons. We savored every bite of steamy stew and followed it with soft, warm cornbread.

Before we knew it, the sun touched the horizon. Uncle Lheotubby left for the village to take his place on the council, and Mother and Pakali cleaned the dishes. When nightfall came, we all went outside to the red post that marked Father's death and remembered him. Mother, Pakali, and Aunt Ohaiki wailed, begging Aba Binili to help my father's spirit find peace. This had become our nightly routine. I had hoped I would become accustomed to the pain by now, but I hadn't.

We went inside and waited for Uncle Lheotubby. I sat down on my bed, resting my chin against my hands. The women talked quietly. I breathed deeply to fight off the rising sadness. It was the quiet times like this that had become the hardest. It wasn't long before Uncle Lheotubby returned.

"What did they say, Lheotubby?" Aunt Ohaiki asked. "What happens next?" Uncle Lheotubby sat down with us on the rug. We all looked at him expectantly. "Well, we have a plan," he said.

"When do we go, Amoshi?" I asked. I stood up and reached for my musket.

"Not so fast, Chula. Our warriors will attack the enemy after the harvest as we discussed before."

"I want to go," I said.

"Yes, I know you do," Uncle Lheotubby said. "So do Mahli, Nashoba, Osi Waka, and Nukni, but some on the council don't think you're ready yet."

"I will be, and I want to prove myself," I said.

"And you will all get your chance to do that," he said.

"How?" I asked.

"We will decide who comes with a game of toli."

I smiled. Toli was more than a game for us. It taught us how to fight as warriors and to work as a team. I often played toli, or stickball, with my friends, but I knew this game would be different. Players could—and likely would—get hurt.

"When, Amoshi?" I asked. "Who will we play?"

"The match will take place after the Green Corn Ceremony, and we will play against our Chickasaw brothers from Chisha Tala," Uncle Lheotubby replied.

"I'm ready to play and to fight," I said.

Uncle Lheotubby looked at Mother. She looked down at her hands and took a deep breath. When she raised her head, she looked at me long and hard. "Chula, you had better listen to chimoshi, and do everything he says," she said. "If you join the raid, I want you to be ready. I want you to come back home again."

I met her eyes with my own, feeling the gravity and the elation of the moment, all at the same time.

"I will, Sashki," I said. "You have my word."

8 THE GREEN CORN CEREMONY

Before we knew it, four moons had passed since Father died. Summer came and the forests were filled with birds and other animals. We had a fair amount of rain and the crops grew nicely. I felt Father's absence often and channeled my still-raw pain into becoming a better hunter. I checked the snares daily and went on hunting trips with my friends or Uncle Lheotubby.

The Green Corn Ceremony was also fast approaching. Each day our minko, Tushka Homa, removed a cane stick from the bundle that marked how many days until the ceremony was to begin, until only one stick was left. The next morning, a runner called out to us as he sprinted past our homes. "The Green Corn Ceremony begins today!"

I rushed outside and watched him run along the ridge toward our neighbor's home. Sunlight was just beginning to break the darkness. He called out again in the distance, repeating the same message to the next household. Each year, we celebrated the Green Corn Ceremony when the corn crop was ready to harvest. We relied on corn for more than just food. Over the next four days, we would give thanks to Aba Binili for the harvest and go through the process of purifying ourselves and our homes. We replaced worn things with new and forgave those in our community who wronged us. Our new year was starting.

I went back inside the house and saw that Mother and Pakali already started to clean. Throughout the day, they would ensure the house and gardens were clean and burn anything old, worn, or broken.

"Chula!" Uncle Lheotubby called from outside. "I'm going to help mend the council house and the other public buildings. Why don't you come with me?"

This was the first time I was asked to help with the repairs that started the Green Corn Ceremony, and I jumped at the chance. It was normally a task for men, not boys. I said goodbye to Mother and Pakali and went with Uncle Lheotubby to the village center.

When we arrived, several men were already mending the grass roof on the council house. Others were preparing the grounds where the hopaii would lead the ceremony. I would miss most of the ceremony, as women and young people were expected to spend much of the next two days at home.

"Lheotubby!" Obiyachatubby called out from atop the council house. "We could use your help patching up this roof."

"You can help me pass up the grass," Michachitubby said.

"Come on, Chula," Uncle Lheotubby said.

We spent the rest of the morning passing bundles of dried grass to Obiyachatubby and two other men. It was my job to take the worn bundles of grass they passed back down and throw them into the fire. We finished the roof as the sun reached its highest point.

"We'd better get home," Uncle Lheotubby said. "The food should be ready by now and this will be my last meal for the next two days."

"How do you do it?" I asked as we walked home.

"How do I do what?"

"I mean, how do you get through the Green Corn Ceremony without eating?" I said. I had never gone more than a day without eating something.

"We just do," Uncle Lheotubby said. "It's part of being a warrior. Fasting instills discipline and reminds us that we rely on each other to succeed. We also cleanse ourselves with the bitter drink, so we can be pure in Aba Binili's eyes."

"Was it hard the first time?" I asked.

"Yes," Uncle Lheotubby said. "But I got through it—and so will you when the time comes."

"I hope so," I said.

"You will," Uncle Lheotubby said with more confidence than I felt.

Outside our home, steam rose from two large pots near the brush arbor. Further away, another fire burned a pile of worn things that Mother and Pakali had thrown out.

"It looks like you've been as busy as we were," Uncle Lheotubby said.

"We have been," Mother said. "Pakali and I almost have the cleaning done, and Aposi and Ohaiki have been cooking."

Pakali was working along the far wall. She pulled a bowl from where it hung by a rope on the wall. She began to cry softly.

"What's wrong?" I asked.

She said nothing. Mother went over to her. She held a chipped brown bowl emblazoned with a red feather in her cupped hands. It was Father's favorite bowl.

"Sashki, can we keep it?" Pakali asked.

Mother hesitated for a moment, looking down at the bowl. "Yes, Pakali, we can. We'll put it right back up where it was."

She nodded and set it down with the other bowls and cups that were good enough to keep and wiped her eyes.

"I think we've done enough cleaning for now," Mother said. "Let's eat before your uncle has to begin his fast."

"I'll get Aposi and Aunt Ohaiki," Pakali said.

"Yakoke," Mother said.

When everyone was gathered, Mother gave us each a bowl filled with stew. We ate as much as our stomachs could hold and shared our hopes for the next year.

•••

Early on the morning of the fourth day of the Green Corn Ceremony, Mother jostled us awake. "Chula, Pakali," she said, "It's the last day. Come on, we've got to get ready!"

The warriors had spent the last two days at the ceremonial grounds. They had fasted, prayed to Aba Binili, and settled lingering disputes and crimes. The old fire was extinguished and the new fire that started the new year was lit. Last night, Mother and the other women had gathered to stand outside the ceremonial grounds to hear the hopaii speak, and the older, prestigious women, including Grandmother, had danced the ceremonial dance with their tortoise-shell rattles worn around their calves. Today we would all participate in the feast and cleansing that ended the ceremony.

We packed the fresh corn, beans, and fruit Mother and Aunt Ohaiki had prepared onto Heloa's back and made our way toward the ceremonial grounds. Everyone from the village was there preparing food and socializing. I saw my friends playing chunkey on the village's clay court.

"Chukma, Chula!" *Osi Waka* called out. "Come join us!"

"Can I, Sashki?" I asked.

"Just don't get into any trouble," she said.

I ran over to the chunkey court where Nashoba was playing against Mahli. *Osi Waka* was rolling the stone.

"Who's winning?" I asked.

"Score is eighteen to seventeen. Nashoba's in the lead."

"Quiet!" Nashoba grumbled. "How can we play if you keep talking back there?"

"Sorry," I said and grinned sheepishly.

"Ready, Mahli?" Nashoba asked.

Mahli nodded.

Osi Waka rolled the polished stone disk onto the court. Nashoba and Mahli raised their spears, trotted forward a step, and hurled them through the air. The chunkey stone slowed, about to topple over, just as the spears began their descent. They stuck into the court near the stone.

Osi Waka ran onto the court with a knotted string to measure the distance between each spear and the stone. "It's close, but Mahli gets the point!"

"That's eighteen even," Mahli said. "Two more shots and your bracelet is mine!"

"I won't be losing my bracelet before you lose that bear-tooth necklace of yours," Nashoba said.

They returned to the edge of the court and prepared for another round. This time Nashoba's spear landed first, but Mahli's spear struck the edge of the stone as it rolled and knocked it forward.

"I hit the stone! That's two points," Mahli shouted. "I win!" He did a quick dance and raised his hands high in the air.

"That was a lucky shot!" Nashoba replied. "I do keep my word, though." He took off the bracelet and gave it to Mahli. "Take good care of it."

"I will," Mahli said, grinning. "And luck had nothing to do with it! That was pure skill—just like hunting a rabbit racing for his hole."

Nashoba laughed, and the two boys shook hands before Mahli slipped the prize onto his wrist.

"So, who wants to play me next?" Mahli called out.

"Chula, why don't you have a go?" Osi Waka said.

"Sure, why not?"

"What will you play for?" Mahli asked, stepping closer.

"I wouldn't mind that bracelet, actually," I said.

"Well, you saw it was a tough match, so I won't take just anything for it," Mahli said. "What will you give when you lose?"

"*When* I lose?" I laughed.

"I'm throwing very well today," he boasted, standing a bit taller and placing his hands on his hips.

"You wish," I said. "*If* I lose, I'll give you two of my blue beads."

"Two of those tired, old blue beads?" Mahli said. "Is that the best you can do?"

Mahli and I both knew he had admired the smooth, round, blue glass beads Uncle Lheotubby had brought me after his last trading trip.

"I tell you what," I said. "I'm so sure I won't have to part with them, that I'll stake four beads against your bracelet."

"Deal!" he said.

He handed Osi Waka the stone. We took our places, and Osi Waka rolled the stone out onto the court. We lifted our spears, stepped forward, and threw them where we thought the stone would come to rest.

As the spears and the stone all reached their destination, we rushed over for a better look. Both spears stood within a hand's breadth of the chunkey stone. Nashoba took the knotted string and measured. "Chula is closer by half a knot," he announced.

I smiled. "It looks like I scored the first point!"

"What a laugh!" Nukni's voice thundered from the sidelines. "Mahli, why are you wasting your time playing this loser?"

I hadn't seen much of Nukni since the night of the council meeting. He'd been making himself scarce lately.

"What's it to you who I play, Nukni?" I said. "Why don't you go pick on someone your own size, and leave us alone?"

Nukni approached me. There was a dangerous spark in his eyes. "It's easy to talk tough when you have your friends around you. Do you expect me to back down because of them? Or, perhaps you expect me to be nice because you lost chiki?"

I could feel the rage beginning to well up from the pit of my stomach as the other boys began to gather around. I closed my eyes and took a deep breath. Nukni had lost his uncle in the raid, too. Surely, he was still grieving like I was, but did he think his loss was greater than mine? This was the Green Corn Ceremony—a time of forgiveness and purification. I had to let it go. I opened my eyes and tried to respond as I knew I should but stopped when I saw his smirk. He was laughing at me! Green Corn Ceremony or no, I let my anger take over. Spear in hand, I stepped closer to him.

"I don't expect you to be nice. You're never nice," I said through clenched teeth. "But you'd better have some respect. Aki was more of a warrior than you—or your dead imoshi—could ever be."

That was all it took to send him over the edge. He took a swing at me, landing a blow just above my ear. Before he could take another, I lunged at him and drove my shoulder into his stomach, knocking him to the dirt. A crowd of boys had gathered around us. One yelled, "Hit him, Chula!" I swung as hard as I could, my fist connecting with his chin.

"You'd better get off me while you still can," Nukni growled. He threw a punch that landed squarely on my right cheek. I held on and kept swinging at him until someone pulled me away.

"Chula!" It was Uncle Lheotubby. He pulled me up as the other boys moved aside. Nukni got up slowly but didn't break his cold glare.

Uncle Lheotubby took my arm and briskly pulled me back to where the women were setting out the food. "Chula, you know full well this is not the time to fight. The Green Corn Ceremony is about forgiving one another and making a fresh start. Why were you fighting Nukni?"

"He deserved it, Amoshi," I said. "He asked for a fight, and he got one."

"Lheotubby, it's time," another warrior called. Uncle Lheotubby looked at me sternly for a moment, then pointed to a spot under a nearby tree. "Stay over there and keep out of trouble," he said.

Still smarting from the punch Nukni landed, I gently rubbed my sore cheek and brushed the dirt from my hair as Uncle Lheotubby walked away.

I plopped down on the ground under the tree. *What just happened?* I wondered. I tried to replay the fight in my head. Nukni and I never liked each other, but this was the first time we actually came to blows. I didn't even hesitate. I let my anger get the better of me. It was because of what he said about *Aki*, I realized. My anger over his death was still so raw, I almost couldn't control it. That scared me a little. Uncle Lheotubby told me once that anger could be a powerful ally if used wisely, but it could also destroy a man if it was not kept in check.

"The meal is ready!" one of the women called out.

Osi Waka and Pakali joined me under the tree. We waited as the women served the hopaii and his assistants first. Then the warriors took their food in order of rank. The women gathered their food next, followed by us young people and children. With food in hand, we sat down next to Mahli and Nashoba on some nearby rocks.

"Amoshi just came back from trading in Charles Town," Mahli told us. "He said it has gotten so crowded that many of the settlers have started moving farther inland."

"Does he think they'll come this far?" *Osi Waka* asked.

"No," Mahli said. "They say they want to stay on the other side of the great mountains."

"I hope they are true to their word and don't try to settle here," Nashoba said.

"Me too," I said. "But one day I think they will. Like Mahli said, the number of people in Charles Town keeps growing, and we don't know how many more live where they come from. They say they only want to trade with us now, but one day they'll want our homes, too."

"I hope you're wrong," *Osi Waka* said.

I hoped so too, but somewhere deep down I knew it would happen. I didn't totally understand how I knew, but I did.

When the meal was finished, the hopaii and two other men approached the fire, praising Aba Binili with arms outstretched. Swan feathers rose majestically from their heads. The hopaii wore white buckskin around his chest and shoulders. The toes of his white buckskin moccasins were streaked with red, and a tuft of wild turkey spurs were attached to the top. Drummers began drumming at each corner of the bonfire. My chest thumped with each beat. "Praise be to Aba Binili, our protector and provider!" the hopaii said.

"Great guardian, you have blessed us!" the crowd replied. "May we follow your will forever!"

The warriors rose from their places and approached the hopaii with their heads covered with white feathers. We watched as they formed three circles around the fire and danced, with the warriors holding a bundle of feathers in each hand. I closed my eyes and thanked Aba Binili for the strength he gave them and us as his people.

The warriors then dressed for war, covering their faces in red and black, and fought as they might an enemy. Uncle Lheotubby raised his dagger as another warrior raced toward him, though he turned it away at the last possible moment to avoid striking his friend. Others fought in a similar way, challenging and charging as they might an enemy, but avoiding the blows that could have ended lives.

When the fighting was done, the hopaii again stood up. "Women, I call on you to join us in the dance," he said. The women stood up and happily joined the warriors in the dance. The three circles around the fire grew and great joy filled us all as the turtle shells strapped to the women's calves rattled. When they finished, the women returned to the edge of the square.

Then one of the hopaii's assistants rose. We moved closer and listened quietly as he spoke. The hopaii's assistant reminded us Aba Binili provided us with everything we needed in this world, and Aba Binili would continue to be with us in the new year. He then urged us to join him for the washing that marked our purity.

I thanked Aba Binili for his love and his strength. When I opened my eyes, I saw Mother walking toward me and Pakali. "Come, Pakali, let me help you."

She covered Pakali and herself with white clay, and I coated my own body—just as everyone else did. Mother then led us toward a group of other women and children and we formed a line. I peeked ahead and saw the hopaii and his assistants at the front. They were followed by our elder men, and then the warriors. The women lined up behind the warriors and then the children followed, with the older children carrying the younger ones. I looked behind me and saw several people straggling along the end. They were those who didn't follow the rules of the Green Corn Ceremony.

"Come, my dear people. Come and cleanse yourselves!" the hopaii called out. We moved in single file toward the creek, where each of us in turn washed the clay from our bodies, signifying our purity.

After we washed, we returned to the ceremonial grounds and the celebration turned to dancing and feasting that continued well into the night.

9 TOLI

With the Green Corn Ceremony behind us, we carried on with our daily lives. Mother and Pakali looked after the rows of corn, beans, potatoes, and tomatoes at home. Uncle Lheotubby and I hunted for deer, checked the snares for rabbits and squirrels, and waded into the creek to spear fish and catch an occasional turtle. We had enough deerskins to keep the traders happy, which helped us stock up on anything else we would need for winter.

Finally, the day of our toli match against our brothers from Chisha Tala arrived. We woke early that morning and traveled to the ball field where the game would take place. Crowds of people from both Ayanaka and Chisha Tala were already there. Mother and Aunt Ohaiki found a spot and settled in next to Grandmother and Pakali.

"Come on, Chula," Uncle Lheotubby said, picking up his

kapucha, his toli sticks, and heading for the other side of the field.

I grabbed my own kapucha and started after him.

"Chula," I heard Mother call.

I turned.

"Play hard, but be careful," she said, the hint of a smile playing at the corner of her mouth.

I grinned at her. "I will, Sashki."

"Fight hard, Chula!" Pakali cried out.

"I will! Just you watch," I said, winking at her.

I had to run hard to catch up to Uncle Lheotubby, who hadn't slowed his gait at all. "Chula, you've seen chiki play, and you know what's involved, right?" he asked as I came up alongside him. "This isn't the same as the toli you've played with your friends. People get hurt."

"Yes, Amoshi, I know." Memories of my father and brother fighting on the field and returning home bruised and sore, but triumphant, flooded my mind.

Uncle Lheotubby stopped and stood silently and solemnly for a moment, studying me. Then he nodded and continued. "Hekiubby is our captain for the match, as he will be in battle. He will decide which of you and your friends will join us on the raid."

I nodded.

"Even if you and your friends play your best, there is a chance you won't go. Some of you may be left behind."

"Yes, but I won't be one of them, Amoshi."

"And what makes you say that?"

"Because I am aki's son, Amoshi," I said. "And because I need justice for his death." My breath quickened and my muscles tensed. I took a deep breath and clenched my fists.

"Just remember, Chula," he said. "There is no greater weapon than humility, no greater threat than pride. Men far stronger, far greater than you have left this field, and the battlefield, in worse shape than they arrived."

"Amoshi, I will show Hekiubby I'm a worthy fighter."

As we waited for our men to assemble, I took stock of the others standing with us at the edge of the field. Nashoba, *Osi Waka*, and Mahli looked small compared to the warriors standing next to them, but they showed no fear. While my friends still wore the long hair or braids of younger boys, most of the warriors sported painted faces and wore their hair in a scalp-lock at the top of their heads. Their brown skin glistened in the morning sun, and most had tattoos, some freshly reapplied for the game. Then I saw Nukni. He had plucked some of the hair from his head in a clumsy attempt to create a scalp-lock.

As we made eye contact, he sneered and tilted his head in my direction. "Look at who we have here," he said. "A little boy playing with the men!"

"Shut up, Nukni," I said. "Unless you want more of what I gave you last time."

He snorted. "You mean that thrashing I gave *you* at the Green Corn Ceremony?" He came in closer and lowered his voice, so only those closest to us could hear him. "And now all is fair play. You'd better watch your back."

"Enough," Hekiubby said, as he walked up behind Nukni. "Save the fighting for the other team. We have a battle to prepare for."

He turned to address the rest of our group. "The other side is strong, and we'll need to play our best if we've got any chance of winning. That means we play as a team. No fighting, no seeking glory for yourselves. Be ready to pass the ball as much as run it, and help those on the team who need it. Let's go."

We made our way onto the playing field to warm up. We gathered our sticks and divided into pairs. "Chula, you're with me," Uncle Lheotubby said.

He put the deerskin ball, the *towa*, into the cupped end of his stick, and we started jogging. "Get ready," he said and passed the towa to me. I reached up and caught it in the cup of my stick. "Okay, throw it back and keep up the pace!" We ran back and forth several times, passing the towa to each other.

"Now something more challenging," Uncle Lheotubby said. We went faster now, almost at a run. "Get ready, Chula." He launched the towa ahead of me. I sprinted forward and dived toward it. It bounced against the side of my stick and ricocheted away from me. I fell hard onto the ground.

"You've got to be ready for anything, Chula. The towa moves fast, and you've got to catch it when it comes your way."

I stood up and took stock of my skinned knees. If that was my only injury of the day, I'd be lucky. "Let's try again, Amoshi!" I said.

Running side by side, I decided to give Uncle Lheotubby some of his own medicine. We passed the towa back and forth a few times, and then I launched it ahead of him so he would have to sprint to catch it, like I did. Uncle Lheotubby surged ahead with his stick stretched in front of him. As the towa fell toward the ground, he leaped into the air and scooped it up like a hawk seizing a helpless sparrow. "*That's* how it's done, Chula!" he called, smiling.

Then Uncle Lheotubby turned back and threw the towa in front of me. I was ready this time, and I bolted ahead, leaped, and caught it in the net of my stick. "Not bad," he said.

Hekiubby trotted toward the center of the field and called out, "Now gather around the goalposts and let's work on defending and scoring."

He motioned to the goals standing at opposite ends of the field. Each was made of two upright posts with a third post lashed in between them, parallel to the ground. They were tall enough for a grown man to walk through, almost like a doorway. To score, players had to either throw the towa through the goal or run through it with the towa cupped in their sticks.

Uncle Lheotubby and I moved toward the goalpost on our left, where Obiyachatubby was already running with the towa, passing it to Anowatubby just as he reached a wall of defenders waiting to stop him. Anowatubby seized the towa with his sticks, smashed right through the line of defenders, and ran toward the goal.

Uncle Lheotubby called out orders as we joined in the melee. "Chula, Mahli, and *Osi Waka*, I want you over here with me. Nashoba and Nukni, you join the defenders—and be sure you defend the goal better than that!" he said, pointing to the warriors who had just let Anowatubby slip through and score.

Uncle Lheotubby placed the towa between his sticks. "Are you ready?" he asked. We nodded our heads. Mahli, Nashoba, and I leaned forward, ready to run. The defenders on the other side crouched low, ready to stop our advance. Without warning, Uncle Lheotubby bolted forward, charging toward the opposite post.

Ninakubby, a respected and powerful warrior, barreled toward Uncle Lheotubby. Just as he lowered himself to strike, Uncle Lheotubby passed the towa off to Mahli, who quickly threw it toward me. Two of the defenders saw the towa sail through the air and tried to beat me to it. I sprinted, pushing my legs to their limit, and reached for the towa. It bounced against the edge of my right stick and dipped into the cup. The goalpost was directly in front of me. Without a second thought, I tilted my sticks back and prepared to throw and score. As I hurled the towa forward, a jarring force crashed into my left hip. I fell and the towa bounced onto the ground ahead of me.

I looked up and saw Nukni standing over me. "I'm sorry, Chula. I didn't see you there," he said with a smirk. I ignored his outstretched hand and pushed myself to my feet.

Nashoba rushed over to us. "Hey!" he said. "We're on the same team. Save the hard hitting for the other guys!"

"It was an accident," Nukni said, trying his best to sound

innocent. I glared at him, biting back the angry retort that threatened to spring from my lips.

Uncle Lheotubby and Mahli came up behind Nashoba. "Are you all right?"

"I will be," I said. But when I tried to move, pain shot through my hip.

"You'll be okay. Let's walk it off," Uncle Lheotubby said. "Nukni, I'm watching you."

Nukni glared sullenly, but held his tongue.

"Put your arm around my shoulder, and we'll get you over where you can rest for a minute," Uncle Lheotubby said.

"Now, what was that all about?" Uncle Lheotubby asked after we'd hobbled across the field and settled on the grass.

"I don't know, really," I said. "He wants to fight, and he always seems to target me, like at the Green Corn Ceremony."

Uncle Lheotubby seemed deep in thought. "I've been told he's really struggling with his imoshi's death. Did you say anything to provoke him?"

"No, I promise!" I said. "He always tries to pick fights, but it's been worse since the hunt. I try to mind my own business, but he doesn't let me. I think he blames me for his imoshi dying."

"You know that's not true, don't you?" Uncle Lheotubby said.

"No." I looked at the ground. There was something I'd been rolling around in my mind for a while. I decided it was time to voice it. "Maybe he's right. And maybe it's my fault Aki died, too. I should have listened to the biskinok's warning. I should have told everyone what we saw."

"Chula, chiki and Nukni's imoshi died because we were ambushed by a band of dishonorable men. It would have happened whether you were there or not, likely even if you had shared the warning. They were both warriors and every warrior knows there's a risk he won't come home. No warrior is immune from death. That is why chishki doesn't want you to join us when we return the attack. You're still young, and chishki and your sister need you."

"Aki's spirit must rest," I said, looking up at Uncle Lheotubby.

Uncle Lheotubby nodded as he gazed into the distance, lost in thought. After a long, silent pause, he put his arm on my shoulder. "Chula, fight as hard as you can today. If Hekiubby asks you to fight, I will not stop you."

"Thank you, Amoshi," I said.

While we watched, players from Chisha Tala poured onto the field. We got into position on the field, too. Two men, one from each village, met in the middle of the field. After speaking with each other, one cried out, "Let's play!"

The men at the center of the field formed a tight circle, with each team facing the other and sticks lifted to seek advantage. One of them threw a deerskin towa straight up, and the game began.

A player from Chisha Tala caught the towa first. We rushed to surround him, but he passed the towa to a teammate downfield before we could stop him. Two of our warriors sprinted toward the towa holder as he took a few steps and passed it again. Our two warriors split up, one chasing the opponent with the towa, and the other blocking his teammates.

As the opposing team passed the towa again, Uncle Lheotubby anticipated the play and smashed into the towa holder before his feet returned to the ground. The towa flew from his sticks, and a swarm of players from both sides battled to gain the advantage.

Anowatubby emerged from the mass of players with the towa for our side. He ran back, throwing the towa to Toklochubby, another of our players, when he saw an opening. Toklochubby caught the towa in midair and bolted toward our opponent's goal. Defenders raced toward him, but he passed the towa before they could stop his advance. Onahubby caught the pass and ran toward the goal,

despite the horde of opposing players on his heels. He threw the towa to another player, who advanced it toward the goal by passing it on to Uncle Lheotubby. The opposing goalkeeper, a large, muscular man with several tattoos, stood ready to defend. Uncle Lheotubby swerved left, away from him, and then swung to the right to pass another defender. Then he hurled the towa toward the goal. We scored!

One of the players returned the towa to the center of the field and tossed it up again. A player from the other team caught it in midair. He turned and ran toward our goal but passed the towa off as Nukni, Osi Waka, and another player caught up with him. One of the Chisha Tala players lunged to catch the towa but was thrown violently to the ground as Mahli collided with him from the side.

As the fallen player dragged himself off the field, another opposing player hurled the towa to a teammate who caught it, turned, and plowed straight past me and Nukni. The opponent sprinted toward the goal, and Nukni and I ran after him. Just as we were about to reach him, the warrior turned back and passed the towa to his teammate to my left. Instinctively, I reached out and intercepted the pass.

I turned, zigzagged past a player from the other side, and ran toward the goal. Not one opposing player, except the goal defender himself, stood in the way. As soon as I was in range, I threw the towa at the goal. It soared through the air and sailed right between the posts!

Uncle Lheotubby jogged past and patted me on the shoulder. The players gathered again in the middle, the towa went up, and an opposing player caught it and took off running. "Chula, go!" Uncle Lheotubby called.

"I've got him!" I said. I ran toward the player and leaned forward, ready to block his pass. I rose up when I saw him raise his sticks to throw the towa to someone behind me, but he quickly pivoted and hurled it toward another player on my left. The towa flew past me and was quickly caught by the other warrior. I sprinted toward the towa with several of my teammates closing in.

The opponent ran toward the middle of the field where the rest of our team stood ready to stop his progress. As I approached, Nukni appeared beside me. "Come on, little boy! You're going to have do better than that if you're going to fight for chiki!" he said and hit me across the back with one of his sticks, nearly knocking me down. He ran ahead.

"Oh, I'll fight!" I said, as I regained my balance. A blaze of anger sparked inside of me, and I pushed aside all the instincts that begged me to control it. Nukni reached the frenzied mob of players before I could and buried himself in. He was so determined to get the ball that he pushed through our own players to get at it. That realization intensified my rage. "You only ever think of yourself, you big, dumb shuk-oshi, you pig!" I yelled.

As soon as I saw an opening, I lunged toward Nukni. My sticks struck his rib cage, and he fell to the ground clutching his sides. I jumped on top of him and began punching. Nukni wailed.

I pounded him until I was lifted by the shoulders and thrown backwards. "Enough!" Hekiubby shouted. "Get off the field!"

"No! I need to play!" I yelled instinctively, as the realization of what I had just done began to sink in.

"Go!" he repeated.

"Chula, now!" Uncle Lheotubby shouted as he approached us.

I turned and stomped off the field without another word. I was still seething with anger. I looked back and saw Nukni slowly getting to his feet. He clutched his ribs with one hand and his bloodied nose with the other. That made me smile just a little. After a few hobbled steps, he seemed to shake it off and joined the rest of the team.

Mother, Pakali, and Grandmother stood up to meet me as I neared them. "Chula—" Mother said.

"Sashki, don't say anything. I know I messed up."

She looked intently at me for a moment, then nodded. "Sit down, Chula." I did as I was told. The match continued until late in the afternoon. Neither team slowed down, and several players left the field bruised and bloody. We were the first to score twenty goals. Of those, Nukni and Mahli each scored one. The other team had seventeen.

Hekiubby and the other team's captain met in the middle of the field and nodded to each other. They turned to face the crowd together. "The fight is over," Hekiubby announced loudly. "Let's make peace over a shared meal."

Many of the women were already preparing pashofa for the hungry players and those of us who watched. We built fires for light and sat together in the warm summer night, celebrating our fellowship.

•••

The next morning, the players from our village gathered at the ball field again. Hekiubby stood with Uncle Lheotubby, Anowatubby, and several other warriors in the middle of the field. As they talked amongst themselves, I knew they were trying to decide which boys, if any of us, were ready to join the fight. Frustration filled me as I thought about how I'd lost my temper with Nukni the day before. He deserved what he got, but now I was sure I would pay the price by being left behind. It occurred to me that maybe that was what Nukni had intended all along.

Anowatubby called for everyone's attention and we all grew quiet. "Chula, Osi Waka, Nashoba, Mahli, and Nukni," he said. "Come forward."

As we approached the warriors, Nukni shot a smug look my way. I thought about smacking him again but refrained. I took a deep breath and turned my gaze toward the warriors. Fear and trepidation grew with every step. Judgement was coming.

We stood in a line, Osi Waka to my left and Nashoba to my right. Mahli and Nukni stood together next to Nashoba. I thought about how I let Nukni get the better of me. He deserved what I gave him, but I could have waited until after the match to deliver it. Because of my impatience, I had likely lost the chance to prove myself as a worthy fighter on this raid. More importantly, I might have lost the chance to avenge my father's death.

"We know that you all want to join us on the raid against the Choctaw," Hekiubby said. "You were all there when they attacked us, and two of you lost loved ones. All of you have worked hard to show that you're ready to join us. You have worked to prove yourselves at home, on the hunt, and on the toli field. We need a strong team. The choices we make now could mean the difference between success and failure, between life and death."

"Remember too that we also need strong people at home," Anowatubby said. "It does us no good to go on the attack while leaving our women, elders, and children exposed. Those who stay behind will be expected to protect the village, a task equally important."

Hekiubby nodded his agreement. "Mahli, you have demonstrated courage on and off the field," he said. "You scored a goal in the toli match and have shown yourself to be an excellent hunter who listens to his elders. We ask you to join us."

Mahli stood straight as a rod and looked down in respect as he nodded once.

"Osi Waka, you are level-headed even under pressure," Hekiubby said. "This is the trait of a good warrior, one who will serve his people well."

"Unfortunately, we just don't believe you're ready yet," Anowatubby said. "You held your own in the toli match but did not shine. It has been the same with your hunting. You are a sure shot, but your caution gets the better of you. You just need more experience, more time."

Osi Waka said nothing but nodded, his shoulders slumped in disappointment.

"Nukni, you are a force of your own," Hekiubby continued. "It is clear that you want nothing more than to be a warrior. You have much to learn, but you have the drive of a wolf. You will not stop until you succeed." He tried to hide it, but as I studied his face out of the corner of my eye, I could tell Nukni feared that he too would be left behind.

"You have proven yourself ready, Nukni," Hekiubby said.

"*But* you must learn to listen," Anowatubby added. "You don't know as much as you think you know. Be humble enough to recognize that, or you or others could get hurt."

Nukni, like Mahli and Osi Waka, looked at the ground in front of him as he nodded his acknowledgment.

"Now, Chula," Hekiubby said.

I thought about Aki's pain and everything I'd worked at to gain the opportunity to avenge his loss. I proved myself as a hunter, and I learned to fire a musket. My failing would come from the toli match. I scored a goal but lost my temper with Nukni. He continued playing as I sat and watched. He was going and now I may not be.

"Your tireless determination shines through everything you do," Hekiubby said. "You may not be the biggest or the strongest in this group, but people underestimate you at their peril." He looked at Nukni, who for a moment returned his gaze.

"But your temper gets the better of you," Anowatubby said. "A good warrior has a cool head. He doesn't lose control like you did yesterday. You didn't even get to finish the game. You, like Nukni, have a soul to avenge. It's hard to keep a cool head when haunted with a restless spirit—but a good warrior manages."

I nodded. My heart dropped as I anticipated what he was going to say next.

"You have proven yourself as a hunter and on the toli field. You have been an honorable brother, son, and nephew in your family. You will learn self-control with time, starting with this raid."

I looked at him in disbelief. "We want you to join us," Anowatubby said.

A flood of thoughts filled my mind as I took in the fact that I was going on the raid. I thought about my father and hoped he would be proud. Even after being sent off the field for hitting Nukni, the warriors wanted me to join them. I saw Nukni looking at me in disbelief and I smiled.

Next to me, I felt Nashoba's posture change slightly. I turned my head to look and saw the disappointment on his face.

"It wasn't an easy decision," Hekiubby said. "We just don't think you are ready yet."

Nashoba wouldn't be going either, I realized. Though sorry for him and Osi Waka, I was thankful that I made the cut. No attack on our people went unanswered, and now I would help avenge those we lost. I wanted nothing more than this, and now I had my chance.

10 THE WINTER HOUSE

T he heat of summer soon abated, and the nights turned crisp and cool. Uncle Lheotubby and I hunted daily now, gliding across the leaves like panthers as we closed in on our prey. We once got so close to a deer, we could almost reach out and touch his fur. Uncle Lheotubby signaled for me to shoot. I pulled back the bowstring, held tight, and released. The deer shrieked, bolted a little way, and then collapsed into the brush. We feasted that night.

The time to attack came before we knew it. Uncle Lheotubby came to find me one afternoon. "We leave in two days," he said. "We need to help chishki and the others prepare for winter before we go."

We began by harvesting the remaining crops from the field. We stored the corn and other vegetables in the corncrib. Mother and Pakali would preserve what they could and take the rest to the market. We ended the day with a brisk swim in the cold creek.

Mother woke us up early the next morning. "Chula and Pakali, why don't you get your things together so we can move them into the winter house?"

I gathered the few items of clothing I had—mostly loincloths for the summer, but also moccasins and a deerskin coat for cooler weather—and laid them into neat piles. I took my musket from its place beside the door, disarmed it, and gently placed it near my clothes. Finally, I took my bow and arrows and placed them next to the gun.

Pakali gathered several deerskin dresses, including a special dress Mother made for her birthday last year. She paused and smiled when she held that dress.

Then she gathered her corn husk dolls onto her bed. Some were large and others very small. She took one of the dolls and paused, staring into its blank face.

"Pakali, let's go," I said.

We got up and carried our things across to the winter house. Its thick, clay-daubed walls and narrow, winding entrance that wrapped around the outer perimeter would keep us warm and protected through the coldest part of winter.

After we moved everything over, Mother prepared our beds with thick blankets to keep us warm at night.

"Chula, go and get some wood so we can feed the fire," Mother said. I went outside to the wood pile and gathered as many logs and sticks as I could carry. I placed them under the arbor, near the large pot Mother used for cooking.

"Now, you two run along so I can finish this," Mother said.

We took some cornbread and nibbled on it as we walked slowly, enjoying the warm sunshine. It would not be long until the cold rains came. We had to make the most of the bright, sunny days while they lasted.

"Chula, let's go into the woods and see what we can find," Pakali said. "Let's look for persimmons. We should find lots of them now." She grabbed my hand, and we headed for the woods.

Pakali was young, but she already had the mind of a good cook. She spent her days with Mother, helping to tend the crops and prepare food for the family. She knew where to find the juiciest blackberries and how to tell good mushrooms from the poisonous ones. Mother was already teaching her how to find plants that could mend stomachaches and cleanse wounds.

We walked along the creek until we found a small stand of trees covered in persimmons. "Look at these!" she exclaimed.

"They look great," I said. "Let's gather as many as we can and take them to Sashki." We began to fill our basket with the small orange fruit. We also took a persimmon or two for ourselves as we picked. When we were done, I was sure we had eaten nearly as many as we put in our basket.

•••

The smell of pashofa greeted us as soon as we reached home. "Just in time," Mother said. "What have you got there?"

"Persimmons," Pakali said.

"Well done," Mother replied. "Set those over there, and I will take care of them later. Take a seat and let's eat." We set the basket of fruit down and sat on woven cane mats. Mother passed us each a bowl of hot pashofa. While we ate, we reflected on our summer blessings. I honed my hunting skills, Pakali looked after the pigs and some of the crops, and Mother had such a good harvest we not only had enough to take us through winter, but also extra to trade for metal cooking pots, cloth, and shot for my gun.

As we sat in silence, I couldn't help but notice a tear sliding down Mother's cheek. I knew she was thinking about Father. We all were, but it did no good to say anything. This was Father's favorite time of year. He loved walking in the woods among the fallen leaves. He always joked that the little people, the *iyakna-sha*, made the leaves fall. He said they pulled handfuls of fiery red, bright yellow, and faded green leaves from the treetops and dropped them onto unsuspecting wanderers in the woods. "If the sudden flood of leaves doesn't scare you, their shrieking cries of laughter will," he said. My eyes began to well up with tears at the memory.

"Chula, it's getting late and your uncle will be here soon. Why don't you tell us a story before he comes?" Mother asked.

"Of course," I said. "Do you have a story in mind?"

"I know one!" Pakali chimed in. "Tell us about the duck and the coyote."

"I think I remember that story," I said and smiled. Mother settled Pakali onto her bed and covered her with a blanket.

"Let me see," I began. "In the woods, there once lived a duck and her five little ducklings. One morning, Mother Duck called her ducklings to the creek so they could have their bath. 'I'm going to sing a song for you,' she said. 'When I finish, I want you all to jump into the water together.'

"The ducklings watched her closely as she sang her song. They pressed their wings against their sides and bent their knees just enough to jump. As soon as she finished, the five little ducklings leaped into the creek and dove beneath the surface. They came up again near the other side and swam back to their mother. She sang the song again and again to them. Each time she finished her song, the little ducklings dove beneath the surface, bobbed back up, and swam around and around.

"Coyote heard the singing and splashing and went to see what was going on. She saw Mother Duck singing to her children. 'You have such a beautiful voice,' Coyote said. 'I would love to bring my children here so you can sing to them, too. But first, tell me how your ducklings stay on top of the water so well?'

"'Aba Binili gives them the power to stay on top of the water,' Mother Duck said. 'If he has given your children the same power, then they too can stay on top.'

"Coyote went to get her children and brought them back to the creek. The little coyotes kept their distance from the water's edge and watched Coyote and Mother Duck with wary eyes.

"'How should I sing the song?' Coyote said. 'Do I call their names as I sing to them?'

"'Oh yes,' Mother Duck said. 'Your children must hear their names before they get into the water.'

"Coyote looked at her children. 'Come closer,' she said. Her children didn't budge.

"'Let me try to help,' Mother Duck said. She turned to the little coyotes and smiled. 'What are your names?' The little coyotes nervously introduced themselves.

"Mother Duck then started to sing for the little coyotes. 'When I get to the end of my song, jump into the water,' she said. She resumed her song and called each little coyote by name. When she finished her song, the little coyotes turned away from the water and ran for home as fast as they could.

"Coyote still tries to sing for her children, but she still can't get them near the water. To this day, the little coyotes run for home when Coyote starts singing her song."

"It looks like your sister is sound asleep," Mother said.

"She is," I said.

"You'd better get ready," Mother said. "Your uncle will be here before you know it." Her voice was thick, and she quickly wiped her eyes with the back of her hand.

"Sashki, I'm going to be fine," I said.

"How can you be so sure, Chula?" she said quietly. "You have no idea what you're getting yourself into."

"I am coming back home, I promise!" I got up and moved over beside her. I put an arm around her and pulled her into a hug. "Aki would want me to do this."

"How can you know that?" she asked.

"Because I feel him here still," I said.

Mother looked up at me. "What do you mean?"

"In the dark of night, I feel the hairs on the back of my neck stand on end," I said. "It always happens just as I start to fall asleep."

She sighed.

"He is a torn man, a man who cannot rest without justice," I said.

She wrapped both arms around me and squeezed me so tightly that I struggled to breathe. "I know. I've felt it, too," she said. "But that doesn't make this any easier."

She let go of me and wiped the tears from her cheeks. "Go. Make chiki proud and come back to me in one piece."

"I promise I will," I said.

I packed my things and prepared my musket. Mother and I looked up at the sound of a soft knock outside. Uncle Lheotubby came in a moment later. "Chukma, Kayohe," he said. He then turned to me. "It's time to go."

I gave Mother one last hug and gently kissed Pakali's cheek as she slept.

"Be careful, son. And remember that your sister and I love you." Mother smiled at me as tears slipped from her eyes.

"I love you too, Sashki," I said. "I'll be home soon."

"I'm counting on it," she said. I gave her another hug, took my things, and left with Uncle Lheotubby.

11 PREPARING FOR WAR

We made our way through the forest. Coyotes bayed at the full moon rising above us, casting its light upon our path. Up ahead, we saw Hekiubby waiting for us, with Ayakubby, the scout.

"It's about time you made it," Hekiubby said.

"Are we that late?" Uncle Lheotubby asked. I could tell Uncle Lheotubby was irritated, but he did his best to hide it.

"You're not the last," Hekiubby answered, folding his arms. "We're still waiting for Onahubby, Mahli, and Obiyachatubby."

"That's them," Ayakubby said, nodding toward the woods behind us.

We turned to see three shadowy shapes approaching us, one somewhat shorter than the others. That, I realized, was Mahli.

We went into the ceremonial house where the hopaii stooped over a large pot set atop a fire, stirring carefully. I glanced around at the other warriors, who took up their places and spoke somberly with each other. I didn't know them all, but some I knew well enough.

Kanahotubby was a friend of my father. They had made several trips together to trade with the English. He was a very good negotiator, but his short temper led even his close friends to mind themselves around him.

"I won't think twice about laying an arrow into any of them," I heard him say not long after the attack that killed my father. "My aim will be true." I knew it would be.

Kanahotubby spoke with Michachitubby and Sahkubby, who both listened intently. Their grim eyes looked straight ahead. Their bodies were covered with tattoos, all telling stories of their blood-soaked victories over fierce and great warriors who opposed them. They were not ones to cross.

Mahli and Nukni, like me, looked as if they were trying to appear as confident as they could in front of the warriors. Mahli quietly stood next to his uncle, Obiyachatubby, his arms crossed and head high like the rest, yet stealing glances at the accomplished warriors. Nukni kept to himself. He seemed to believe a sullen and disinterested face was the best imitation of a warrior. I began to say something to Mahli about him, but Hekiubby stepped forth, and all eyes went to him.

"Warriors," he said with a voice that rang like iron. "The time has come for us to hunt and kill the snakes who struck us." He peered at each of us, eye to eye. I resisted the impulse to look down. "You have sharpened your arrows and prepared your muskets. You have trained, prayed, and said your farewells. It is time to deliver justice and peace for our fallen friends."

Hekiubby cried out the call of war, and we joined him. We followed him in a circle around the outside of the house three times, led by his cries, Ayakubby's strong singing, and the beat of Obiyachatubby's drum. Our spirit of vengeance caught and spread like a sudden fire, burning through us, heating our souls. We cried out louder still, perhaps loud enough to reach the homes of our enemies, where the terror of our vengeance would strike their hearts like a plague and make them shrivel. For a moment, I thought I saw my father in the shadows, encouraging us on. I smiled and my nervousness faded.

Hekiubby at last called the dance to a halt, and we went back inside. The hopaii was there waiting for us, holding a great shell cup in his hands. We fell silent.

"Come," he said, "let us pray, and then you shall take of the beloved drink." He paused, lifted the cup high and turned his eyes upward. "Beloved Creator, we pray for your strength and justice, so that we may repay those who unjustly struck us, your servants, and give rest to the beloved warriors taken from us. We lament each moment they're gone. Guide our warriors and protect them, so they return having brought peace to our beloved fallen. They honor you."

He lowered the cup to his chest, returning his eyes to us. "Remember always that no warrior goes alone. Aba Binili watches over our beloved, even in the darkest of nights."

Murmurs of agreement and approval rippled through the room.

"A warrior must be pure," the hopaii said, "fully apart from the cares or concerns that might turn his heart away from battle and give the enemy a path to defeat our beloved." He paused, still holding the cup with the bitter drink glistening inside. Only his eyes moved across us. "No warrior should join this fight if his mind is burdened with such cares. It is a solemn duty, not a matter of shame, to stay behind for this reason. Are there any whose rightful cares might—?"

He did not finish the question. He looked around the room, his eyes seeming to probe each warrior as they slowly passed over us.

No one answered, and no one moved. My eyes turned hard and I felt a sense of strength rush through me. The time for vengeance was coming. My path was ahead. I was one with the warriors.

"Then come," the hopaii said. "Drink. Be purified. Remember our beloved who fell before the enemy you will strike. Purify your spirits, so that you may be fit to avenge them."

We approached the hopaii, Hekiubby leading the way with Uncle Lheotubby right behind him. When it was my turn, I heaved the moment the bitter drink touched my lips. I took a great gulp of it into my mouth and forced it down with a hard swallow. It felt like a black, bitter river rock, angrily shouldering its way down to the pit of my gut. Unwanted tears poured from my eyes. My stomach rebelled. I clenched my jaws. For a moment, I could have sworn I saw my father standing in the shadows, although my sight was turning blurry.

"You will find rest, Aki," I muttered. "I promise." I moved my tongue around, trying to clear the bitterness from my mouth.

Uncle Lheotubby patted my back, which was no help. "Okay, Chula?"

"Yes, Uncle, I'm fine." I must have sounded like I was being strangled.

"Glad to hear," he said. I recognized the tone of dry, grim humor shared among warriors. "You'll have a lot more before we go," he added. He sounded a little like it was something I should look forward to.

I coughed, too preoccupied to notice he was speaking to me like an equal. The news about having to take more of the bitter drink made my stomach jerk sideways. "M-m-more?" I tried to sound casual.

He nodded, as if it was common knowledge. "You'll have nothing else until sunset for the next three days."

My stomach bucked like a fresh horse. "I'm—I'm not sure I—I

can kee—keep it down," I stammered. I was trying hard to keep my lips pressed together.

"You won't," he promised, unperturbed. I noticed he wasn't having the same trouble with it that I was. "The drink purifies mind and body," he added. "It brings us all closer to Aba Binili."

I struggled to keep my arms from wrapping around my stomach. "What happens if I can't drink any more?" I gulped.

He turned serious, eyeing me levelly. "Then you can't go with us," he said. "It would mean you're not ready."

"I am ready, Uncle," I said, doing my best to stand up straight. It was hard, but I hoped that I managed to look straight and strong.

"Good," he said. "We're watching you."

True to his word, he watched me run outside, unsteadily, no longer able to resist my stomach's command. At least I wasn't first. Other warriors who had already begun threw up with the purpose and ceremony of veterans. I held my stomach, buckled to kneel, and retched. I gave myself credit for at least paying enough mind not to get in anybody's way.

When I was done, Hekiubby took me by the shoulders and directed me back inside, where the hopaii awaited us with impassive, expectant eyes, holding toward me the shell again filled with the bitter drink. It was all I could do to keep from moaning.

•••

"Chula!" Hekiubby shouted.

It was dark still—and cold. I turned beneath my blanket. I heard others muttering in protest.

Hekiubby sounded hoarse but would not be put off. "We must go soon. Up, and get ready."

I got up and joined others who gathered at the fire. I sat next to Mahli. After three days of fasting and drinking the bitter drink, he looked as spent as I felt.

"Are you ready?" Mahli whispered, glancing around as if afraid to be heard. Warriors are ready for war every moment and did not need to be asked. We both knew that.

"As ready as I'm going to be," I said. "It's time to give Aki's spirit the rest he deserves." Suddenly, I felt alive. It must be the effects of the cleansing, I thought. Even though I was tired, I was ready to fight.

"Same for me," Mahli said. He closed his eyes for a moment and shuddered, as if shaking off a spirit of childish fear. "I'm ready."

"You're not scared are you, little boys?" Nukni asked, already taunting us. He walked our way, stretching himself up in an attempt to exaggerate how much taller he was.

"No more than you," Mahli said, sighing as if he couldn't care less what Nukni thought.

"'No more than you,'" Nukni mocked. "Scared little boys."

"Enough," I said calmly as I stood up. "Or I will silence you." Before I would have shouted such warnings, but now, like a warrior, I spoke them quietly, as if everyone knew their truth.

"You can try," he challenged, squaring his feet.

I held my gaze at him.

"Enough!" Hekiubby barked in our direction. "Save it for the enemy."

I continued holding Nukni's gaze. He did not back down, either. I understood. No warrior backs down.

Hakalotubby stepped between us, his eyes flashing with a quick anger that seized our attention. "All three of you are acting like little boys," he snarled. "Little boys stay at home with their mothers." He huffed like a bear and, after taking a hard look at all three of us, walked away.

I turned my attention to Hekiubby, not at all concerned that Nukni still stood in place, ready to fight. He was not worth risking my chance to join the raid. I was not a little boy anymore and wouldn't let myself act like one.

"Get ready," Hekiubby ordered. "Make your final preparations."

"Come, Chula," Uncle Lheotubby said.

He pulled out two leather pouches. The vermillion and black paint I knew were in those pouches symbolized honor and death among warriors. I had seen Father and Uncle Lheotubby wear these colors many times and had longed for the day when I would join them. Now the time had come. The colors were mostly made from plants found in the forest, although we valued the vermillion that we got by trading with the English. The paint was made by mixing the color with spit and a special bear grease kept by one of the elder women. It was easy enough to put it on, but the paint would hold its place, even if a warrior fell into the water.

"You've seen this done before, right Chula?" he said.

"Yes, I saw *Aki* preparing his face a few times," I said.

"Good," Uncle Lheotubby said. He opened the pouches and held them in his right hand. "First, I want you to take the black paint from here and draw a line across my cheeks, going just beneath my eyes. Start at the ridge of my nose and stop just before you reach my ears."

I dipped my finger into the smaller pouch and rubbed it against the cool black paint. I touched Uncle Lheotubby's nose and he closed his eyes. I rubbed the paint beneath his right eye, dipping into the pouch as needed, and then did the same beneath his left. "Make sure you leave a straight line across each eye," he said.

"I did," I said. "Both lines are as straight as arrows."

"Good job," he said. "Now take the vermillion paint and cover everything above the black lines on my face."

I dipped my finger into the pouch of red paint and brushed the paint above the black marks as he instructed. I added more paint until the upper part of his face shined in vermillion. With his painted face, copper ear pieces, and the tattoos of outstretched eagle talons on his chest, Uncle Lheotubby was ready.

"Well done, Chula," Uncle Lheotubby said. "Now it's your turn." He pulled a sharp knife from his pouch.

"What's that for?" I asked.

"We need to shave your head first," he said. "Come closer and look at my feet." Uncle Lheotubby took some of the hair from the front of my head in one hand and brushed the knife blade across it with the other. A tuft of hair fell onto the ground. He took another tuft and cut it as well. He continued until he trimmed all of the hair on the top and sides of my head. He then took a small piece of razor-sharp obsidian and shaved the short hair so that I, like him, was nearly bald; only enough hair to form a knot at the top remained. A breeze brushed across my head and I shivered.

"I left your scalp," he remarked, like he'd done me a favor.

I smiled, a little, like I supposed a warrior might. It wasn't easy. I could still feel blood trickle from at least a couple of nicks. I knew better than to say anything, even if he had sliced me to ribbons.

"If it's a scalp you want," I answered, practicing at not smiling while doing so, "I promise to get one for you later."

Uncle Lheotubby flicked the back of my neck. He, like most warriors, seldom laughed when preparing for battle, even at the funniest of jokes. This was as close as he would come.

"Now raise your head and close your eyes," Uncle Lheotubby said. He covered my eyes with black paint and extended a line of black paint across each cheek. Uncle Lheotubby then covered the upper part of my face with red paint so that I now looked like him. When he finished, he tilted my head a little this way, then that, perhaps to make sure he'd done it right.

"Like your father," he said, just like that, and turned to his pouch.

I sat still, doing my best to ignore a chill.

Uncle Lheotubby didn't smile, but I could see the pride and strength in his eyes. "Now you are ready," he said.

I looked around at the others. Each peered straight ahead, grimly focused on the task before us. A few warriors, like Chufatubby and my uncle, bore odd scars of war on their cheeks and heads made clear by the vermilion bound into them. I could also see differences between the warriors who came from the village, like myself and Uncle Lheotubby, and the hardy, mysterious sorts like Michachitubby and Sahkubby, who dwelled in the forests. We all wore black stripes across our cheeks just below our eyes, but the forest people covered the lower part of their face with vermillion paint, below the black stripes, rather than above them as we did.

We all turned toward the door when the hopaii entered, dressed in his finest, like at the Green Corn Ceremony. He held a small wooden box almost pressed to his chest. It would go with us.

"We are ready," Hekiubby declared. There was not so much as a rustle from the rest of us.

The hopaii took an earthen jar and a gourd from the box, set them aside with ceremonious care, and turned to fill the familiar shell with the bitter drink once again. As he did, he prayed. "Aba Binili, you have protected your people since the first days. You have given us our Homeland and the finest foods, and you taught us how to live. For this, we give you thanks."

"Thank you, Great Provider," Hekiubby said. We repeated his words.

"Our enemies attacked us," the hopaii continued. "They took some of our beloved. Their spirits plead to us for justice and peace."

"Hear us, Great Protector," we responded.

"Our fighters have prepared themselves. They have cleansed themselves with the beloved drink. Lead them to the enemy and protect them with your strength."

"Lead us and guard us."

The hopaii lifted up the shell and closed his eyes. "You have been purified by the beloved drink and are as one. You go under the strength of Aba Binili. Come, take one more drink before you leave."

We gathered before the hopaii. Hekiubby took the shell and had the first drink. He then passed it along. When my turn came, I swallowed without wincing. I thanked Aba Binili that I found it easier to drink than I did three days earlier.

The hopaii looked us in the eyes, one by one. "You are now ready." He poured some of the drink into the earthen jar, dipped the gourd into it, and shook it over each of us, covering us with the bitter drink. He put the gourd and jar back into the wooden box and held it out before Hekiubby.

"Take this as a sign that Aba Binili is with you all. Respect and protect it, for what it carries is sacred and beloved," the hopaii said.

Hekiubby took the box. "We will protect it with our lives. It will not so much as touch the ground."

"You will need a trusted helper," the hopaii continued, following the ritual of old. "One who will carry it, and to give the drink to fellow warriors when they need it. Whom do you choose?"

"I choose Ayakubby," Hekiubby said.

Ayakubby said nothing, but turned to offer his back, upon which was strapped a leather harness, worn from its many journeys. Hekiubby bound the box within its straps and checked that it was held firmly in place.

"Protect it, and Aba Binili will protect you," the hopaii said.

I knew the box was sacred. Uncle Lheotubby told me about it before, warning that only the two selected to watch over it could carry or even touch it. He did not say what would happen to anyone else who dared to try.

Hekiubby turned to us, his eyes alight with impatient fire. "Warriors, our fallen brothers and sisters call us to vengeance. Our guns and arrows burn on our backs. Let's leave and take glory." He and Ayakubby let out cries that would terrify the stoutest enemy and sprinted through the door.

We chased after, sending up cries of our own, with each cry longer, higher, and louder than the one before it. Morning songbirds celebrating the sunrise turned away to flee into the woods. We moved at a swift run up to the water's edge.

At last, the journey I longed for, for so long, was about to begin.

12 ON ENEMY LAND

Five canoes carved from cypress trees rested nearby, ready for our use. Hekiubby and Ayakubby set off first, and the rest of us followed closely in two rows side-by-side.

I watched the murky water break across my oar as we picked up speed. The thick scent of last night's rain lingered even as the sun broke through the scattered clouds. "Take care with that oar, Chula," Uncle Lheotubby said. "Water moccasins love swimming in water like this. You don't want one on the other end of your oar."

We rounded a steep-banked bend in the creek and the farms of Ayanaka faded among the trees. "This could be our last glimpse of home," Uncle Lheotubby murmured quietly. I nodded slowly.

The waters widened. We maneuvered our way past logs, sand-banks, and the occasional tree rising out of the water, as the current carried us on. Turtles huddled together along the shore to bask in the sunlight. I gazed into the water as I paddled mind-lessly. On one level, of course, I knew that we might not make it back. Brave people could die, just like my father did. But, for the first time perhaps, the realization that I myself may have seen my home, my mother, and my sister for the last time began to sink in.

"Chula, are you all right?" Uncle Lheotubby asked.

"I'm fine, Uncle," I said.

"Your thoughts seem to be elsewhere."

"I'm just trying to take in what you said about us seeing home for the last time."

"It might be," Uncle Lheotubby said. "You didn't realize that?"

"I guess I did, Uncle. It just seems a lot more real, a lot more final now."

"Of course it's real, Chula. You wanted nothing more than to avenge chiki's death, and that means killing someone else. They will do their best to kill us first."

"I know, Uncle," I said. My mind numbed and I could think of nothing more to say.

"Chula?" he said after a few moments of silence.

"Yes, Uncle?" I said.

"You need to think about whether you really want to do this," Uncle Lheotubby said. "It isn't too late if you want to go back home. There is no shame in that choice."

I took a deep breath. "Yes, I'm a little nervous," I said. "But I'm more scared of not going. I can't get the sight of my father's torn spirit out of my head. Every time I close my eyes I see him in the shadows."

"I understand, Chula."

"I owe him this."

Uncle Lheotubby patted my shoulder. "You are indeed a brave fighter and I have no doubt that your father is proud of you," he said. "Just remember, no matter how hard the coming days might be, Aba Binili is always with us. He will guide us and, if he so chooses, he will call us home. It is all in his hands."

I nodded.

We continued our journey in silence, focused on our fight. The creek twisted and turned its way southward. We pushed ahead, all through the night.

•••

My arms and back ached after yesterday's long journey. Today would be just as tiring. The leaves on the banks glittered with dew in the morning sunlight, and pockets of mist rose above the water. A large heron watched us warily. As the sun continued its ascent, the mist cleared and birds flew overhead.

With a nod from Ayakubby, Hekiubby used hand gestures to signal that we were nearing the end of this leg of our journey. At this point, stealth was of utmost importance. We were entering enemy territory and did not want to alert anyone of our presence.

We came around a bend, and Ayakubby signaled that we would walk from here.

We got out of our canoes and filled them with big river rocks to sink them. Then we set off on the leaf-covered trail. Hekiubby and Ayakubby led, followed by Obiyachatubby and Mahli. Uncle Lheotubby and I followed them and the others walked behind us. Sahkubby and Kanahotubby brought up the rear. We each kept an eye out for danger, and every man spoke in the lowest whispers or with signs.

"We should reach their village by sunset tomorrow, if we're quick," Ayakubby whispered.

"So we move quickly," Hekiubby answered.

We trotted through woods for most of the day. The trees stretched their yellow-leafed branches high above us. The air around us was thick and still. Beads of sweat dripped along my cheeks. A dry thirst threatened to overwhelm my throat when I saw a stream flowing ahead of us.

"Let's refill our pouches," Hekiubby gestured when we reached the stream. We kneeled at the water's edge and leaned in for a drink. I cupped my hand, filled it with water, and took a sip. The cool water soothed my dry mouth, but I noticed a faint stench in the air. I looked up at the others.

"Something is dead upstream," Onahubby whispered.

Sahkubby signaled us to follow the stream, we would stop for water later.

"Quickly," Hekiubby urged with his hands.

The stench grew with each step.

"That is surely the smell of death," Uncle Lheotubby whispered.

Sahkubby went ahead of us along the trail and stopped.

"What is it?" Onahubby asked with hand signals. "A dead deer?"

Sahkubby shook his head and pointed to the right, along the water, and gave a sign: "A man."

There in the trees stood four wooden poles supporting a platform of branches covered with bark and leaves. A wasp flew past my ear. I froze.

"Come, Chula," whispered Uncle Lheotubby. He pulled my hand, urging me to walk slowly and follow.

We walked past the platform. I held my breath. I looked up and immediately wished I hadn't. Swarms of wasps and flies buzzed around a rotting, eyeless demon who stared back at me. Flesh hung limply from the side of what once was a face. White and red lumps bulged where eyes once rested, and beetles walked in and out of his mouth. Bones, muscles, and flesh in the shape of arms lay at his sides. Another swarm of flies hovered below, near the water's edge.

I nearly choked on the thick stench. Memories of my brother and those we lost flooded into my mind. Those we lost while away from home were lain on platforms like this and, over time, they would rest in this way as well. I couldn't breathe. My brother, a fierce warrior, would have faced this same fate. Uncle Lheotubby reached toward me and covered my mouth.

"Don't say anything," he signaled. "We don't want anyone to know we're here."

I nodded slowly.

Nukni retched. I turned and saw him cough into the grass. "Keep yourself together," Sahkubby hissed into his ear. "Now's not the time to get sick," he signed.

I saw Mahli doing his best to keep his composure. "Is that a Choctaw?" he signaled to Hekiubby.

"Yes," Hekiubby replied in kind. "We are on their land now."

We continued upriver and refilled our pouches. "We move on," Hekiubby gestured. "It's getting late."

We made our way closer to the enemy's village while the sun drew to the horizon. I thought about the dead man on the platform. He was once full of life, but now he lay silent and still, just like Aki and my brother. He, like them, once looked after his family and struck fear in the hearts of his enemies. I wondered whether his soul found peace like my brother, or if he wandered the spirit world in pain like Aki. I prayed that he found peace.

When darkness fell, we stopped at a clearing and set up camp without a fire, to avoid detection. We took a handful of dried corn from our pouches and ate just enough to calm our stomachs and keep our energy up.

But I could not get the sight or the thought of the Choctaw's corpse out of my mind. I wondered how long he'd been lying up there. I remembered the time, long ago, while I was still little, when Mahli and I sat near the warriors and listened to them talk about the dead around an evening fire, in a time of peace.

"In a year," Chufatubby had said, somewhat loudly I think because he wanted Mahli and me to hear, "a man will be little more than bones, hair, and the clothes he was given."

Sahkubby turned to look right at me. "Ask chimoshi what happens next," he had said. The others laughed. Uncle Lheotubby grimaced.

"What does happen next?" I had to know.

"You've never heard about the bone pickers?" asked Uncle Lheotubby.

"Yes," I said. "Aki said they would come for me if I didn't do my chores."

Everyone laughed again.

"Well, I can see why you might think so, but no, they won't go after you for not doing your chores," Uncle Lheotubby said. "I have to give chiki credit, though. I wouldn't have thought of that!"

His reassurances didn't do much to persuade me that Aki had been wrong.

"I still do my chores!" I asserted.

Mahli nodded in agreement.

"Well, that's good," Uncle Lheotubby said, "but no bone picker was going to get you."

"Are they real, though?"

"Yes."

"What do they do, then?" I asked.

"When it's time to take the remains down, the bone pickers climb onto the platform and peel away any skin, muscles, or guts that remain on the bones. They keep their fingernails long and sharp, like bear claws, for this very purpose." Uncle Lheotubby raised his hand, curled his fingers like a claw, and grimaced.

Mahli and I had held our breath, listening intently to every word.

"Should I continue?" he asked.

"You already started, so you may as well finish," Anowatubby said ruefully.

"When they're done, they wipe the sticky remains from their hands onto the ground. Then they put the bones, one by one, into a special deerskin pouch and return it to their village. The family gathers, pay their respect, and place the bones to rest with their ancestors."

Mahli and I had glanced at each other and then quickly looked away at the fire.

Now, tonight on the raid, without a fire, in the darkness under the trees, I struggled to get those images from long ago out of my head. I could hear the faint bays of coyotes somewhere deep in the woods. Each cry lifted a torn, bloodied face out of the darkness. It was my father's. His face hovered so close to mine I could feel my breath bouncing against what once was warm flesh. It rose and fell with each haunting call until I finally heard nothing and saw only blackness.

13 BLOOD SPILLS

Hekiubby shook my shoulder as he passed by me. I struggled to open my eyes. It was still dark and damp on the forest floor. Birds called out in the distance.

Hekiubby and Anowatubby took their places in the middle of us.

"Today's the day for revenge!" Anowatubby gestured.

"We should reach their village by nightfall," Hekiubby indicated. "We must go now."

I got to my feet carefully. Rays of sunlight poured across the forest floor. The trail banked to the left down a steep hill and away from the stream. Thorn-filled shrubs lined the trail, and many of the trees were laced with poison ivy.

"This could be our last day," Sahkubby whispered to Chufatubby. "Make the most of it."

Chufatubby sneered. "They are cowards, not warriors!" he signed.

"Even cowards will fight when they are cornered," Sahkubby whispered. "Remember why we're on this mission."

Chufatubby scowled. We all knew Sahkubby was right, but no one wanted to admit it. It was far easier to imagine coming home a hero than not coming home at all.

•••

We raced along until the light in the forest faded. We reached a valley. Across it, fields of cut cornstalks stretched as far as we could see. Wooden houses, much like our summer houses, stood here and there. In the distance, I saw two women tending a field near one.

Anowatubby signaled to Hekiubby. "Should we attack now?"

Hekiubby nodded. There seemed to be just enough daylight to see what we were doing without the whole village seeing us first.

"They owe us six souls," Anowatubby whispered. "Let's settle this."

Hekiubby summoned me, Mahli, Nukni, Chufatubby, Obiyachatubby to come close so he could whisper and sign, "All of you, stay here. Guard us so they can't surprise us from behind."

"No," I whispered. "I came to repay aki's killer, not stand by and watch."

"I'm not here to watch, either," Nukni added.

"You won't," hissed Hekiubby, pulling our heads close. "When we shoot, every enemy who hears it will know what's going on and will come. We need a strong team to get us out again."

Uncle Lheotubby pulled me close. "We have fought and you have not. We've seen what happens when raids go wrong. We need you to do this."

"I want revenge," I whispered again.

"You'll get your chance."

My heart sank. I knew the decision was made.

I took a deep breath and paused. "Okay, I'll stay here," I said.

Nukni opened his mouth, but Uncle Lheotubby stopped him with a look, clearly saying, "You'll keep quiet if you know what's good for you."

"We have to go," Hekiubby signed.

We grasped our muskets and laid our bows and arrows across our backs. Hekiubby led the others down into the fields, creeping low in the shadows. They snuck past the home of the women we had watched and slipped out of sight.

Crickets and locusts sang their loud evening choruses, but we still spoke in the lightest of whispers.

"What do we watch for?" Nukni asked.

"We will know as soon as the enemy does," said Obiyachatubby. "The others will shoot at the first men of fighting age they see."

"If they're lucky, no one will see them," said Chufatubby.

"And they'll go on to find others," Obiyachatubby said.

"I'm not sure Aba Binili himself could get away with killing six people without being seen," Chufatubby said.

The sound of a musket firing tore through the air. Chufatubby signaled us toward the woods.

Nukni, Mahli, and I backed away into the nearby trees, ducking instinctively at the sound of a second shot. Chufatubby and Obiyachatubby loaded their muskets and charged toward the gunfire.

And then I heard Nukni shout.

I turned to see an enemy warrior right next to me, pressing a knife into Nukni's shoulder, which was already oozing blood. Without a second thought, I grabbed the warrior and threw him to the ground. Out of nowhere Mahli pounced onto the warrior's chest and drove his hunting knife into his neck. By the time Obiyachatubby and Chufatubby returned, the enemy was dead.

There was no time to celebrate. Another shot whistled over our heads. In an instant, Obiyachatubby fired back through the trees, and I saw an enemy warrior fall to the ground.

Without a word, Chufatubby guided Nukni into the tall brush, took out a cloth, and wrapped it tightly around his shoulder. He yelped.

Chufatubby and Obiyachatubby quickly covered Nukni's mouth. Obiyachatubby leaned in close to Nukni's face with a finger pressed to his lips.

"Take deep breaths," Chufatubby whispered and pressed the cloth against Nukni's shoulder. He seemed to be bleeding less now, but I figured one of his bones was likely broken or cracked by the enemy's knife.

Two more shots rang out in the distance, then others somewhat closer.

Chufatubby gave us a look that told us the action was headed our way.

Nukni looked around as best he could, trying to grasp the situation, his eyes flashed with pain and confusion.

Chufatubby and Obiyachatubby looked to me, simultaneously communicating a sense of urgency. I let out a deep breath and nodded. I would stay with Nukni. We would remain the lone rear guard.

More sharp shots came to our ears. Chufatubby, Mahli, and Obiyachatubby rushed down the hill. The sun neared the horizon and the shadows stretched as all fell oddly silent.

Nukni sighed.

I listened to the rise and fall of crickets chirping in the woods around us. I thought about my assignment to stay behind with Nukni—and why I'd agreed to it. I couldn't fully explain it even to myself. It just seemed like the right thing to do. If I was the one who was hurt, I wouldn't want to be left on my own, especially with the enemy closing in. And the warriors still needed someone to guard the way out.

"I think I've lost my chance for revenge," Nukni muttered glumly. "Amoshi may never find peace."

"I may have lost mine, too," I said. "I see aki's spirit often. He suffers."

"I see amoshi," Nukni said. "His thirst for vengeance grows by the day."

I shrugged. I figured we should stop talking. I still hoped I hadn't missed the chance for vengeance I'd fought so hard to get. Father's spirit demanded peace, and I needed it, too. I hadn't slept a full night since he died.

A twig snapped behind us. Nukni raised his head and tried to hide the pain that the movement caused. I caught a glimpse of someone coming up the trail below us. I stepped back into the shadows with my musket, signaling Nukni to stay quiet. He worked his way deeper into the tall brush, grasping his knife.

I crept between the trees, trying not to trip as I struggled to see in the twilight. I could make out a tall man coming up the trail toward us. He looked around carefully as he walked, watching for the slightest movement.

I heard a rustle in the brush. I froze. My heart skipped when the man turned toward the sound, pulling a long-bladed knife from a sash on his hip. He raised it, looking about for the source. I had to do something before he found Nukni hiding there in the brush!

I raised my musket and stepped out of the shadows. "Stop," I said coldly.

He stopped but did not lower his blade. I inched closer, my mind racing. If I fired and missed, it would put me and Nukni in danger. Even if I hit him, I didn't know for sure if he was alone.

"Lay down your knife and keep still."

The man tossed his knife into the grass. I walked a little closer, trying to stay quiet and out of reach. "Who are you?" I asked.

"Your worst nightmare," he said. Though he spoke the words in Choctaw, our languages were similar enough I understood him. "Come closer and fight me like a real warrior."

I inched around him until I could see his face, and he could see mine. He laughed. "You're just a boy," he said. "What are you doing here?"

"I am here for revenge," I said. "One of you killed aki as we hunted last spring."

"And how do you know he didn't deserve it?"

I pulled back the hammer on my musket.

His smile quickly faded. "Do you really think attacking my people and killing us will give your father peace?"

"Aki will deal with the enemies I send to the spirit world tonight," I said. "He will find peace."

"But will you?" he asked.

We looked into each other's eyes for a moment.

"I'm about to find out," I said finally.

The flicker of a torch appeared down the trail, behind the man. I kept the musket pointed at him but stepped back into the shadows, my heart racing. *More of them*, I feared.

A young boy came trotting up, a torch in his hand. "Father!" he called. "Wait for me!" The man turned to look, startled. The boy was no bigger than Pakali. He looked up at his father, then at me, not comprehending what he saw. He grabbed his father's arm.

"Get behind me, son," the man said. He looked back to me. "I will fight you but spare my son." The boy tightened his grip.

A chill came over me. The man's face looked just like my father's, resolute but full of pain and emptiness. I fought back tears. Images of Father and me standing together filled my head.

The sound of gunfire rose in the distance again.

The man and his son stood still. "If you're going to shoot, boy, you'd better do it now," the man said in broken Chickasaw.

I wanted to shoot this man and ease my father's suffering, but I couldn't. He was a father with a loving son. I couldn't take him from this boy as the Choctaws had done to me. I recognized this boy, too—innocent and afraid. I knew he would do all he could to find me and get revenge for his dead father, just as I had tried to do for mine.

The gunfire grew nearer. Men shouted in the field below. "Go," I said.

"You'd better go, too, while you still have a chance," the man said. He swung the boy into his arms, turned, and disappeared.

I ran to Nukni. He huddled in the brush, clutching his shoulder. He looked confused, as if I'd woken him from a deep sleep.

"Chula, did you get them?" he asked.

"No."

"Why not?"

I didn't want to tell him what I had done. Nukni already thought I was weak. If I told him, it would prove him right, and everyone else would think so, too. "I was ready to fire, but I heard gunshots," I explained. "I didn't want the enemy to know where we are, so I let him get away. I figured we might be caught if they heard me shoot."

Nukni nodded in agreement and appreciation. It was a half-truth, but he believed it. The cries and gunshots grew fainter. I could only hope it meant we were safe.

We sat still in the dark. The long, tense silence finally ended with the sound of rustling leaves and footsteps coming near. I could see dark figures moving about in the woods. I raised my musket and steadied it against a tree, ready to fire if I needed to.

"They're coming," Nukni whispered. He blinked and gripped his knife again.

"Quiet," I hissed. The rustles grew closer.

Nukni gathered himself to get up, grimacing. We both feared not being able to escape the enemy warriors, and I figured there had to be many. If we got caught, they would make us wish we were never born. I touched Nukni's good shoulder as a signal, and he understood, circling behind me so I could defend him.

I heard a whisper and I knew. It was Hekiubby. "Where did you leave them?"

"Here, in the brush," Chufatubby answered.

I stood up so they could see me.

"Chula," Hekiubby whispered, and I returned the greeting. "Nukni?" he asked.

Nukni pulled himself up next to me.

Obiyachatubby came to look at Nukni's shoulder. He couldn't lift his arm. Hekiubby took some dried yarrow from Ayakubby, crushed it over the wound, and covered it with a bandage.

Nukni took it stoically, but it looked like it took much of his strength. I looked around at the other warriors and could see none was missing.

We heard shouts from far off and could see torches lit in the valley below.

"We go, now" Hekiubby signaled.

We left as fast as we could. The path out was difficult, but we kept up a fast pace until we got back to our canoes.

14 MERCY

We paddled our canoes homeward. My gut lingered behind, with the man and his son and the choice I made. I had done the inexcusable. The enemy had attacked us and killed my father and several others. They showed no mercy, yet I gave mercy to them. After waiting so long and doing all I could to take revenge, I took none. I had no courage to do what I had to do. I was weak.

I closed my eyes and again saw the warrior and his son, together, staring down the barrel of my musket. The warrior stood taut, ready to meet his fate. His son did not. I could still see the fear in his eyes.

An angry whisper swept over the water to my ears. "Mahli!" Obiyachatubby hissed from the boat next to ours, "Lift that oar! Keep up!"

Mahli jerked, nearly dropped his oar in the water, and quickened his pace.

Obiyachatubby kept after him. "What's wrong with you?" he whispered between clenched teeth, keeping his voice low so it would not carry to the banks and be heard.

Mahli made no answer, setting his jaw firm and his eyes forward, bending to paddle into the stream and, it seemed to me, against something only he could see. I thought I knew what it was.

Hekiubby spoke, but quietly, seeming to feel a little more at ease after the good distance we'd made. "Mahli has earned a name and an honor," he said with grim pride. "He met his enemy and overcame him. Ah! Perhaps he's so quiet because he sees the spirit of that Choctaw."

Uncle Lheotubby glanced at Mahli. "Perhaps," he murmured, as if to himself. "That's part of life after you kill in battle."

"I've lost count of how many spirits haunt me," Hakalotubby muttered. He sounded not at all bothered to say so.

Kanahotubby nodded his head as if to add he couldn't count the spirits who haunted him either. He looked solemn, just as he always did.

The man I almost killed, and the boy who clung to his side, were still in my mind's eye, also. They stood frozen in that moment when I'd held my musket ready to kill the man. I was his enemy. I could have been his killer, too, and made his son fatherless, like me. Or I could have killed them both, then and there. I might have had to. *Would they haunt me, like the warrior who haunts Mahli?* I wondered. My gut churned faster and faster, a flood of guilt swirling into a storm of confusion. It was almost too much to bear. I had come to win peace for my father but failed. I let him down in a way I could reveal to no one. To make things worse, I felt cold, unwelcome relief that an enemy's spirit would not haunt me. That meant my father's would. For the rest of my days, I would still see my father being laid into the ground. His spirit would forever pursue me, demanding justice and relentlessly reminding me that I was weak.

I glanced at Uncle Lheotubby's impassive face. He cared for me and watched me grow. He prepared me to become a warrior, but he could not make me become one. The burden of my betrayal bent my soul like grass beneath my feet. I could say nothing.

"It gets better, I suppose." Mahli said, in a low, quiet tone like the others. His eyes turned hard and edgy, like knapped flint.

"You get used to it," Obiyachatubby replied quickly, as if to be done with the matter.

We paddled through the chilly night. The sun was beginning to rise through the dark mist when we reached the junction of Chiwapa and Town creeks. "Almost home," Hekiubby declared.

"We did well," Anowatubby remarked. "We came together to avenge the loss of our beloved, as was our duty. Aba Binili heard our prayers, and he answered."

"Yes," Chufatubby agreed. "He guided us and guarded us while we paddled into enemy waters and walked through enemy lands. We avenged those we lost, without losing anyone."

"Almost lost one," Onahubby said, glancing at Nukni.

Nukni waved them off weakly, clearly not wanting that sort of attention. "I'm all right."

"You will recover," Hekiubby said.

I thought of Nukni and then Father. "Amoshi," I asked Uncle Lheotubby quietly, "do you think he'll get better?"

"It's in Aba Binili's hands," Uncle Lheotubby said, shrugging and nodding. "But, yes. We'll see how his shoulder heals."

"He's a mean one," I said, low enough so Nukni could not hear. "But he's a good warrior."

"He has a chance to be one," Uncle Lheotubby corrected me, not sounding so persuaded as I tried to seem. We turned our attention back to the rest, who were beginning to share their praises.

"Ayakubby," Hekiubby called out, "you led us through creek and trail to our enemy."

"It was my honor," Ayakubby answered.

"Kanahotubby," Hekiubby put in, "you killed two at a great distance. As soon as Sahkubby pointed them out, you shot an arrow at one and then the other, before he had a chance to work out what happened."

"They'll have plenty of time to work it out in the spirit world," Kanahotubby replied.

"That they will," Hekiubby agreed. "And after we snuck into the village, we tested our luck when a musket ball hit the dirt next to Onahubby's foot."

"That was a mistake someone won't be making again," Onahubby observed.

"True," Hekiubby said.

•••

The sun rose higher over Chiwapa Creek, and I saw trails of smoke rising above the trees ahead.

"Not much farther," Chufatubby said.

"Ayakubby should be there by now," Hekiubby said. "He will make sure everything is ready for us to thank Aba Binili and celebrate our success."

"We should start celebrations now," Anowatubby said and let out a cry of triumph, at the top of his lungs. The rest joined him, offering up cries of victory and thanks. Even Mahli joined in, but not me. I wanted the others to know how grateful I felt for our victory, but I could not lift my voice to fly upward and mingle with theirs. I tried to make the same grim smile of triumph as they did but felt like I was only making a face. I just wanted to dive into the cold water and not come back up.

We passed a group of children bathing. They shouted to us,

smiling, pointing, and laughing. A house appeared, chickens cackling and hogs grunting nearby as we paddled past. An old man carrying a bundle of pelts over his shoulder came out of the woods, eyes wide with surprise.

"You're back," he called out.

"Yes," answered Hekiubby with a fierce, victorious grin. "And we repaid our enemy."

The man lowered his bundle. "They killed my son," he said, his voice trembling. "Tell me my son can now have peace."

"Yes, your son has his peace," answered Hekiubby, with grave respect. "We have delivered justice for him and all the others."

The man rushed into the water, wading toward us, hands held high. "I cannot thank you enough for what you have done." Tears ran down his leathery cheeks.

"It was our privilege," Kanahotubby said.

We continued, passing other houses and the large, flat hilltop where traders gathered. Upon it people bustled back and forth with deerskins, pottery, food, and baskets. Children ran and played, and a group of men huddled together near the bank, deep in conversation.

"Home," Uncle Lheotubby remarked, simply.

"Nukni should see the alikchi," Hekiubby said.

"I can walk," Nukni grumbled. He was beginning to sound like his irritable self, so I figured he might be feeling better already.

We walked up the bank, whooping while Hekiubby shouted the victory song. We returned with no man lost, and the village celebrated around us, drawing together and circling like a big, formless dance. I felt lost and alone in the middle of it.

The alikchi made short work of Nukni, touching up his wound with herbs and declaring him able to join Mahli, me, and the warriors to begin the customs of the three days of separation. Still, he would be taken in isolation to heal and complete purification for the wound he suffered.

I went to see him later. I found him sitting on a bed, his head down. He kept a fresh plaster of herbs pressed to his shoulder.

"Nukni," I said.

He raised his head to look into my eyes. "Well, Chula. I think perhaps you saved my life."

I shrugged, not feeling at all worthy to talk of myself. "You will be a great warrior," I said. I didn't want to try to think of anything else to say. I had just spent three eternal days in ceremony and purification that I had done nothing to earn, even if I put myself into it, trying to match the real warriors around me.

Its ending was a bitter relief, and not a full one. Throughout the ceremonies, I kept my eyes to the ground, terrified that Father's spirit would arise before us all to accuse and betray me. I often closed them to keep tears from falling, but it did no good. Each time, I saw the warrior and the boy grimly staring back in the darkness, close enough to touch them. I knew that, even though they lived, their spirits—or those of demons who masked themselves with their faces—were there only to torment me of my failure. Perhaps they would haunt me forever.

I left with Uncle Lheotubby for the final leg of our journey home. I felt exhausted. Finally, seeing the thatched roof of our winter house in the distance brought some relief.

"We made it," I said, breaking the silence between us. Uncle Lheotubby had been quiet all the way home.

"*Shhh*," he whispered. "Let's surprise chishki."

I resisted an urge to run to the house and instead walked slowly behind Uncle Lheotubby. My heart leaped, for the first time in what felt like ages, when I saw Pakali come outside. "Pakali!" I shouted, no longer able to contain myself. I know I sounded hoarse, almost limp with exhaustion.

She jumped up and down, beaming with joy. "Chula!" she

shouted, flying toward us. "Sashki! Chula's home!" She slammed into me and hugged me so tightly I could barely breathe.

Mother rushed outside. "Chula, Lheotubby!"

"Yes, safe and sound," Uncle Lheotubby said.

"I'm just thankful you're home," Mother said. She joined my sister to embrace me.

"You'll suffocate him!" Uncle Lheotubby laughed, now sounding more like an uncle than a warrior.

"I'm so glad you're home. Lheotubby, why don't you come in?"

Uncle Lheotubby smiled but shook his head. "No, I need to see Ohaiki first."

"Of course. Why don't you both come here to join us for a meal? You can get Aposi to come as well."

"I will," Uncle Lheotubby said and turned toward his home.

It surprised me that Mother urged me to tell her all about the raid. I feared that if I began to speak of those things, I would break down. Then, from somewhere deep within, a spirit, quiet and firm and so old and true that I could not help but trust it, nudged me to continue. I began to speak. I told her about our journey into enemy lands. I described how we found the dead man on a scaffold and how the raid began. I told her about the heroism of the elder warriors and how Nukni was stabbed. I said nothing of the enemy warrior and his son. I said nothing about my failure.

I finished and looked at Pakali. Her face shined with wide eyes and a beaming smile.

"I'm glad you made it home, Chula," Mother said and pressed my hand. "Chiki would be proud of you."

To my surprise, I felt lifted, not ashamed. The spirit that encouraged me to speak gave me hope that, while life would never be easy, it could be livable. I was still young, it told me. My doom was long yet to come, and much still lay in my hands.

•••

I looked back at the crowds. Mother, Grandmother, Uncle Lhe-otubby, Aunt Ohaiki, and Pakali all smiled at me. Tushka Homa, our minko, and Hekiubby stood ahead of us next to the minko from Chisha Tala on the chunkey court. They both stood before Mahli. Tushka Homa raised a large eagle feather, held it above Mahli's head, and then passed it to the other minko.

"Today, we celebrate the moment a boy becomes a man," the Chisha Tala minko proclaimed. "We start our lives as children, and we play, learn, and focus on ourselves. A boy becomes a man when he puts others first, even when doing so threatens his own life. A man swallows the fears he faces. He takes strength from his fear and he perseveres."

"Mahli was among those who were attacked by the Choctaws last spring, and he helped lay to rest those we lost," Tushka Homa said. "He knew the dangers of going on a raid, but he risked his life to restore justice for his people."

"Mahli kept his courage throughout the raid," Hekiubby said. "Mahli's courage shined in the heat of battle when an enemy war-rior struck from behind. Mahli pounced on the enemy and took his life."

"By your bravery, you have become a man," the Chisha Tala minko said. The Chisha Tala minko lowered the eagle feather upon the top of Mahli's head. "From now, you will be called Pis-amontubby, for you killed your enemy at first sight." The Chisha Tala minko turned Mahli so that he faced us and smiled. Everyone looked on with quiet appreciation and pride for him.

"Congratulations, Pisamontubby!" Hekiubby shouted. "You are a warrior, and I look forward to fighting alongside you again."

Obiyachatubby then joined Pisamontubby and the others. "Well done, Pisamontubby," he said. "You have done me a great honor, as your uncle. You will make your people proud."

Men whooped and women joined in with exultant cries of war, but I was lost in my own thoughts. I was proud of Mahli—or Pisamontubby—but part of me wished I was the one who made my uncle proud. As Uncle Lheotubby and others went forth to offer their congratulations, I felt like a failure. I saw Tishkila, Osi Waka, and Nashoba smiling and my sense of failure grew. Even Nukni let out a great whoop, although I knew he found it hard to do. I understood.

I thought back to the moment I threw the enemy warrior from Nukni, but it was Mahli who finished him off. *Why didn't I kill him?* I asked myself. I could have been the one standing before the minkos to become a warrior, the one who earned the pride of his family and his community. I couldn't blame Mahli for my failure. I also had a chance with the warrior in the woods and his son, but I did nothing. *Worse yet, I let them live!* I thought.

A hand touched my shoulder and I jumped. I looked up and saw the hopaii. "Chula, why do you look so distant?" he asked.

Deep inside I felt the same spirit that had nudged me to tell Mother about the raid begin to stir. I knew it was time to admit what happened.

"I let my family down," I said.

"What makes you think that?" he asked.

"I had two chances to give aki the peace he longed for, and I missed them."

"But chiki did find his peace," the hopaii said.

"How do you know?" I asked. Now I was confused.

"I saw him," he replied. "As a hopaii, I help the spirits who seek my guidance along with those who are still living. I know chiki is with your brother, and they have found their peace."

"But I should have been the one who gave him his peace," I said. "I didn't."

"Your father has nothing but pride for you," the hopaii said. "He saw your determination to do what was right, and he knows that you were with the warriors who gave him justice."

"I hope you're right," I said.

"Chula, what if being a warrior is not the path that Aba Binili set for you?" the hopaii asked.

Again, confusion set upon me. "What are you saying?" I asked. I must have sounded angry. "That I'm too much a coward to fight, to kill an enemy? No, I won't let that be my fate!"

"Your fate is not to be a coward, Chula," the hopaii said reassuringly. Then he smiled. "Your path is far brighter than that."

"What do you mean?" I asked.

"Yours is a path that few can take," he said. "You will help your people hear the will of Aba Binili. You will give them strength to follow it."

"How?"

"If you truly want it," he said, "you will become a hopaii, a servant of Aba Binili. You will hear Aba Binili's voice, and the voices of the spirits. You will pray, and you will seek his favor in times of need, for the people."

"A hopaii?" I was surprised. "Why do you think this is my path?"

"Because the spirits already speak with you," he said. "They've chosen you because of your compassion for others. Did you not feel it when you chose to let the enemy warrior and his son live?"

"I thought it was weakness," I blushed and turned my eyes from him. "I looked into their eyes and I felt no choice but to let them live."

"Perhaps Aba Binili told you to let them live," he said. "Perhaps they too have a role to play for him."

"And that's why you think I should be a hopaii?" I asked.

"That's part of it," the hopaii said. "You have also seen the little people, the *iyaknasha*. They've spoken with you. They trust you."

"How do you know that?" I asked.

"Because I speak with them, too. One of them told me how he met you after ch*i*ki died," the hopaii said. "They don't trust most people. Only they choose who can see them. Most know them only from stories they hear."

"I would never have expected such an honor," I said. "That Aba Binili would want me as his servant."

"I strongly believe he does, Chula," the hopaii replied. "Our people need his guidance now more than ever. The Choctaws grow more restless by the day. They will attack us again. The French and British will continue to grow in number and strength, as will the devastation they leave behind. Dark days lie ahead. The people will look to you, and to Aba Binili, to guide them through. They will seek your council as they face times as they never imagined. They will look for hope, and you will need to give it to them. The minkos and the warriors will look for guidance, and they will come to you."

My mind filled with thoughts, fears, and hopes as I tried to make sense of the hopaii's words. I was not to be a warrior, but a hopaii. My heart raced with awe. I gazed across the crowd around Pisamontubby and the minkos. I felt pained by their smiles and their laughter, not because of envy of Pisamontubby, but because I knew that pain and sorrow would soon come to them all, if the hopaii was right. They would one day come to me for hope, for comfort. I prayed to Aba Binili, asking that he give me the faith to hear his will, the wisdom to understand it, and the strength to guide our people through the times that would come to pass.

•••

Later that evening, when we'd all returned to our homes, Uncle Lheotubby, Aunt Ohaiki, and Grandmother joined us for a celebration meal. As we ate, I listened quietly as my family talked. Mother and Pakali joked and laughed, but Mother's shining eyes betrayed the tears of gratitude she tried to contain. I realized how close I came to never seeing her or Pakali again, never again sharing a meal, never laughing, never playing or hunting.

I stepped away to fill my chest with crisp night air. A few coyotes yapped in the woods nearby. Crickets chirped drowsily. I turned my eyes up to the stars and gazed at them a long time, until a giant bear materialized among them, looking down at me. Shadowy silhouettes of deer bounded past, running and playing amidst the stars.

Behind them, a large, powerful warrior stood with his bow at the ready. Vivid vermillion paint covered his face and a large black streak swept beneath both eyes. Three white feathers rose above him, glowing in the night. He turned toward me, lowered his bow and smiled, with the grim smile of a warrior. My father turned and a second, younger warrior appeared at his side, with the same grim smile. It was my brother.

"Aki," I whispered. "Anukfi, Brother." They turned away, and with the animals, faded into the darkness between the stars. A quick light, a fuchik maleli, whisked across the horizon, leaving a fading streak behind.

"Thank you, Aba Binili," I whispered. "Thank you for your mercy and love."

I looked toward the house. Mother and the others still laughed and talked. My spirit began to feel cleansed of guilt. I went back inside.

"Chula, you're smiling," Mother said.

"I saw Aki," I said. "He is well."

GLOSSARY

The Chickasaw language (Chikasha anumpa) is an important part of our culture and part of what makes us uniquely Chickasaw. For centuries it was an oral language, not written down formally until the 1970s. Today there are two main spelling systems used by the Chickasaw Nation, so you may see variations in spelling. Chikasha anumpa includes some sounds that are not found in English. Vowels that appear in italics are called nasal vowels, which means they are pronounced with a slight "n" sound at the end of the vowel sound. For example: *a*ki is pronounced ahn-ke, and pak*a*li is pronounced pah-kahn-le. To show possession, such as "my" and "your" in Chikasha anumpa, different prefixes are added to the base word. For example: *ishki* means "mother," but *sashki* means "my mother."

Aba Binili (ah-bah beh-ni-lee): name for the Creator, means "He who sits on high"

a **ki** (ahn-ke): my father, or Father

alikchi (ah-lik-che): doctor or healer

amoshi (ah-moh-she): my uncle, or Uncle

*a***nukfi** (ahn-nak-fe): my brother, or Brother

An*o*watubby (a-nohn-wah-tub-be): a traditional warrior name, means "He walked around there killing" or "He killed again"

aposi (a-poh-se): my grandmother, or Grandmother

Ayakubby (ay-ah-kub-be): a traditional warrior name, means "He killed one far off"

biskinok (bis-keh-nok): a bird that Chickasaw warriors believed brought warning of impending military disaster or defeat.

ch*i*ki (chehn-ki): your father

chimoshi (che-moh-she): your uncle

chiposi (che-poh-se): your grandmother

chishki (chish-ke): your mother

chishkosi (chish-koh-se): your aunt

Chufatubby (chu-fah-tub-be): a traditional warrior name, means "He killed one of them"

chukma (chook-mah): good, often used as a greeting similar to hello

chula (choo-lah): fox

fuchik maleli (fooch-ik mah-le-le): a comet

Hakalotubby (huk-loh-tub-be): a traditional warrior name, means "He heard him and killed him"

Hekiubby (he-kee-ub-be): a traditional warrior name, means "He killed the one standing up"

heloa (he-loh-ah): thunder

hopaii (hoh-pah-e): prophet

*i***ki** (ehn-ke): father

Imonubby (em-oh-nub-be): a traditional warrior name, means "An enemy came to his house and he killed him"

imoshi (e-moh-she): uncle

inkoni homa (in-koh-ne hohm-ah): red skunk

iposi (e-poh-se): grandmother

ishki (ish-ke): mother

ishkosi (ish-koh-se): aunt

iyaknasha (ehn-yahk-nah-shah): woodland spirits known as "little people"

Kanah*o*tubby (kah-nah-hohn-tub-be): a traditional warrior name, means "Killed someone"

kapucha (ka-pooch-ah): stickball sticks

Kayohe (kah-yoh-he): a historic Chickasaw female name, its original meaning is unknown

Lheotubby (thle-oh-tub-be): a traditional warrior name, means "Chased and killed"

mahli (mah-le): wind

Michachitubby (me-chah-che-tub-be): a traditional warrior name, means "He was far from the enemy and killed him"

minko (mehn-koh): leader

nashoba (nah-shoh-bah): wolf

Ninakubby (ne-nah-kub-be): a traditional warrior name, means "Killed at night"

nukni (nuk-ne): male, also a boy's name

Obiyachatubby (oh-be-yah-chah-tub-be): a traditional warrior name, means "It was evening and he killed"

Ohaiki (oh-hi-ke): a historic Chickasaw female name, its original meaning is unknown

Onahubby (oh-nah-hub-be): a traditional warrior name, means "Killed after daylight"

*o*si waka (ohn-se wah-kah): flying eagle

pak*a*li (pah-kahn-le): flower, also a girl's name

Pisamontubby (pe-sah-mon-tub-be): a traditional warrior name, means "Killed at first sight"

Pisatubby (pe-sah-tub-be): a traditional warrior name, means "Saw and killed"

pashofa (pa-shoh-fah): a traditional Chickasaw dish made with cracked corn and pork

Sahkubby (sah-kub-be): a traditional warrior name, means "Caught up and killed"

sashki (sahsh-ke): my mother, or Mother

shuk-oshi (shuk-oshi): pig

t*i*shkila (tehnsh-ke-lah): blue jay or jaybird

Toklochubby (tuk-loh-chub-be): a traditional warrior name, means "He killed two of them"

toli (toh-lee): stickball

Tona (toh-nah): a historic Chickasaw female name, its original meaning is unknown

towa (toh-wah): ball

Tushka Homa (tush-kah hohm-ah): a traditional warrior name, means "Red warrior"